KEN
HOLLISTER

KRIS MICHAELS

Copyright © 2023 by Kris Michaels

All rights reserved.

No part of this book may be reproduced in any form or by any electronic or mechanical means, including information storage and retrieval systems, without written permission from the author, except for the use of brief quotations in a book review.

❀ Created with Vellum

HOLLISTER
AND
A LONG ROAD HOME SERIES

CHARACTER LIST BOOK 4 - KEN

Book	Character Name	Spouse	Child (c)	Legend
1	Andrew "Drew" Hollister VI (h)	(2) Genevieve "Gen" Wheeler (s)(w)	Andrew "Sev" Hollister VII	(#) age order
The Long Road Home Series - Searching for Home - a crossover with Hollister and Guardian				(s) sibling
	Scott "Vader" Evers (h)	Ciera Gordon / London Evers (w)	Cody Allen Evers (a)*	(h) husband
2	Dr. Ezekiel "Zeke" Johnson (h)	(2) Stephanie Howard Johnson (s)(w)		(w) wife
3	(1) Declan Mason Howard (s)(h)(p)	Melody Ann Erikson Howard (w)(p)	(1) Scott (s)(t)	(p) parent
			(2) Jared (s)(t)	(c) child
The Long Road Home Series - A Home For Love - a crossover with Hollister and Guardian				(t) twin
	Alexander Alex "Bull" Thompson (h)	Kayla Marie Bryce Thompson (w)		(a) adopted
4	(1) Kendall "Ken" Zorn (s)[e]	Samantha "Sam" Quinn [e]		(d) deceased
				[e] engaged

(a)* Cody is Ciera's biological child. Scott adopted him when they got married.

CHAPTER 1

Ken Zorn shifted behind the wheel of his Ford Expedition and leaned forward, squinting. *No, just ... no.* He hit his blue lights and chirped his siren. As the old tractor in front of him swerved radically, he winced. The thing maneuvered to the shoulder of the road and stopped. Ken pulled up behind it and put his vehicle in Park.

He wasn't calling it in. Lord, he'd never live it down. He approached the tractor and gestured for the driver to cut the engine.

After reaching down and shutting it off, Craig Johnson looked up and greeted him. "Hi, Deputy Zorn." The twelve-year-old licked his lips and glanced at his ten-year-old sister, Hailey, and their dog, Buck, beside him.

"Craig, what in the blazes are you doing driving on the highway? If someone wasn't watching coming over one of those hills, they could rear-end you. Does your dad know you're driving out here?"

Both of the children shook their heads. "No, sir. He's asleep. He worked all night," Hailey said, petting the Border Collie as she spoke.

Craig nodded, adding, "It's his birthday today. We wanted to get him a cake and maybe a present. We've been saving up our allowances. We have thirty-seven dollars."

"You were driving the tractor into Hollister? That's fifteen miles." Ken leaned against the engine's casing.

"Yes, sir, but we didn't have everything to bake a cake," Hailey said. "Since Momma died, it's been hard on Daddy. And us. We miss her." The little girl's eyes misted up, and Buck leaned into her and licked her face.

Ken scrubbed his brow. God, the priceless hearts of children could slay him. "Okay, how about this? I'll get your dad a cake and a card you can sign. You turn this thing around and get home. I'll follow you to your turnoff."

"You'd do that?" Craig stood up and pulled a wad of crumpled dollar bills from his pocket.

"You keep that, okay? We can settle up later. I don't know how much it'll cost." He wouldn't be taking anything from them. Ken put aside two hundred dollars a month to help those who needed it. It was his way of giving back to the community.

Ken glanced down the road and rolled his eyes before smiling widely. Well, it was something they could laugh about for the rest of the week. Sam was right on time in her highway patrol vehicle. As she pulled up behind him, he could see the smile on her face was as big as the South Dakota sky. She clearly got the humor of the situation. For the last six months, they'd developed one hell of a friendship based on their jobs and similar sense of humor.

"He likes chocolate," Hailey said, bringing his attention back to the children. "Do you think they have a chocolate cake?"

Sam walked up beside him and winked. "Need help on this high-risk traffic stop?"

"Nah, Craig and Hailey are heading home."

"That's right." Craig nodded. "Deputy Zorn is going to get Dad a birthday cake."

3

"And a card," Hailey added, still petting Buck. The dog's tongue lolled out as he stared at Sam.

"Is that so?" Sam glanced at the little girl. "Is there anything I can do to help?"

She shook her head. "No. Daddy's sleeping. He was up all night with the milk cow. She was really colicky, but Dad says she'll be okay now. We've already cleaned up the house." Hailey answered in a way that damn near ripped out Ken's heart. Those kids were so freaking pure.

Sam glanced at him. "Well, I tell you what. I'll head into Hollister and make sure Deputy Zorn gets what he needs, and then, we'll bring the cake and card out to you."

"Thanks." Craig smiled briefly before deflating. "But if Dad sees you, he'll know we took the tractor."

Ken nodded. "He needs to know, Craig. No matter how good your intentions were, taking the tractor on the highway was the wrong thing to do. You know that, right?" Both heads dipped up and down as they stared at him. "We can tell him together when we come out to the ranch. I think the cake and the card will soften him up." Sam smiled at him as he reassured the kids.

Hailey smiled. "Chocolate, right?"

"You bet, even if I have to bake it myself," Sam promised the little girl.

"Okay, let's turn this thing around. I'll follow you back to your access road. And, Craig, if I see you driving on the highway again, I'll call it in. It's illegal, and you could have caused an accident. You're supposed to be taking care of Hailey and Buck, not putting them in danger."

"Yes, sir. I didn't think about that," Craig said and looked over at his sister. "I'm sorry, Hailey."

"You didn't know." His sister stared up at him. "It's okay."

"This time," Samantha said. "But you have to have a license to drive on the highways. Are we clear on that?"

"Yes, ma'am," they answered together.

"Crank this bad boy up, turn it around, and I'll follow you back to your place. We'll be out in a couple of hours," Ken directed.

"Yes, sir." Craig reached down and started the ancient tractor. The thing rumbled into a loud, cranky purr, and Craig put it into gear.

Ken and Sam stood in the middle of the road, stopping the nonexistent traffic until the five-point turn was completed, and the tractor trundled down the road.

"Lunch?" he asked his work partner and friend.

"Sure. Let me stop in and see if Allison has any cakes made. Then I'll meet you at the diner."

"She usually has a couple frozen for last-minute things like this. Here." Ken reached into his wallet and pulled out a fifty. "For the cake and the card."

"That's okay. This is my treat." Sam winked at him from under the brim of her highway patrol hat.

"Well, the next time we stop a couple of kids and need to buy a birthday cake, I'll treat."

"Cool, or you *could* buy me lunch," Sam said with a laugh as she walked to her patrol car.

"Deal!" Ken called back to her as he got into his SUV. He turned off his blue lights, put on his hazards, and idled down the road after the children. It took almost ten minutes, but they finally turned into the small ranch's access road and pulled into a pasture, angling the tractor straight for the barn. Ken drove onto the gravel road and parked, watching as they slowly made their way through the field and pulled the tractor beside the big red barn. Buck jumped off, the black and white ball of energy bouncing around the small tractor as Craig got off and helped Hailey down. Ken watched until they made it across the wide expanse from the barn to the house before putting the car into reverse and backing out onto the highway.

His phone pinged, and he glanced down at the text.

> Score! Chocolate cake and card. You're buying lunch.

KEN PULLED over on the side of the road before responding. He'd never text and drive. He'd seen too many accidents and senseless fatality reports to do that.

> Perfect. On my way.

HE SMILED, ensured the road was clear, and headed into Hollister. The smile on his face had been etched there since Sam had started working in the area. They met up once or twice a week. Usually, once for lunch and once somewhere along the road. They'd visit and talk about careers, their aspirations, and the stupid crime of the week. There was rarely a shortage of those tales. Craig and Hailey, as sweet as they were, fell into the top three that week. God, if someone had been speeding … it could have ended horribly. He'd had his share of fatality wrecks, and he never wanted to process another.

The diner looked full when he pulled up and parked by Sam's patrol car. He got out and headed into the little building that had become the default meeting place of Hollister.

"Hey, Ken," Alex Thompson greeted as he entered. Alex ate lunch at the diner almost every day, and Ken usually sat with him, but not this day.

"Alex." He nodded a greeting. "Busy day?"

"Always." The man chuckled. "Old engines always need TLC." The mechanic had taken a load off Phil when he'd started working at Phil's garage before Christmas last year.

"Where's Kayla?" Ken looked for Alex's fiancée. Phil's niece and Alex had hit it off almost immediately, and they were good for each other. Ken felt a twinge of jealousy, not about Kayla but about the love that was so obvious between them. He'd had epic failures in the romance department between his long history with Allison and the several flame and burn-out relationships with women he thought were right for him. Boy, had he been epically wrong. Somehow, he never found the right person. Hell, he'd pretty much stopped trying.

"She went into Rapid with her Aunt Sarah to get more fabric." Alex reached for his milk. "Busy day?"

Sam spoke from her seat in the booth she'd claimed for her and Ken deeper in the diner. "High-speed pursuits and top-secret missions."

Ken laughed and clamped Alex on the shoulder. "Don't believe everything you hear."

Alex snorted. "I never do." He went back to his food, and Ken nodded to a few of the regulars on his way to the seat Sam had saved for him.

"What's this about a high-speed pursuit?" Edna Michaelson had twisted halfway around in her booth to ask the question. The town's self-appointed know-it-all was harmless but definitely in everyone's business. Her cronies, Belinda and Doris, stared at him, waiting for an answer.

"I'm afraid Sam was pulling your leg, ladies. No high-speed pursuits today." Ken turned to sit in his booth and popped his eyes at Sam, who smiled as she took a sip of her iced tea.

"But what about the top-secret mission?" Ryan Conklin, the ranch foreman from the Hollister place, asked from across the diner. Every last person stopped what they were doing and looked at the booth where he and Sam sat.

"You answer them." Ken reached for his cola and took a drink.

Sam glanced over at Ryan. "The Johnson kids asked us to get their dad a birthday cake. They had no way of getting to town." She turned to Ken and lifted an eyebrow in a *There, take that* fashion. He smiled and shook his head.

"It's Lawrence's birthday?" Edna slapped the table. "This is the first one since Bridgette died, right?"

There was a rise in the conversation around them. Corrie came out of the back of the diner with two specials for him and Sam. Roast beef, mashed potatoes, beets, and a salad.

Sam looked at the plate. "This is an entire side of beef."

Corrie laughed. "Almost. I have to-go containers on standby. Need anything else?"

"Nope, and I have the bill today," Ken said.

"You got it." Corrie moved away and cleared dishes while chatting with people.

Sam took a bite of her beef and moaned a low, quiet mewl of pleasure. The sound reverberated through him, and he lifted his eyes and stared at her. The look of exquisite pleasure on her face did things to his body that should never happen in public. She opened her eyes and blinked. "Damn, did I make that sound out loud?" she whispered.

"You did." He nodded.

"Well, now you know what I sound like when I'm happy. Deal with it," she quipped quietly and took a bite of her potatoes.

Samantha Quinn had hooked him like no other woman. Even Allison. Hell, he couldn't remember what the fascination with Allison was when Sam sat across from him. Sam was happy, fun, open, and charismatic. She was sharper than a fine-edged knife and not one to let anything slip by her. He genuinely enjoyed spending time with the woman. They spoke the same language. It was refreshing not to have to dumb something down or constantly stop to explain the law to someone. Not that he minded talking with the people in his care. He loved his little community, but sometimes, it was lonely. Hell, Sam had it all. She was so damn pretty, even with her hair pulled back tight and shoved into a bun at the base of her neck. He wondered how long her hair was when it was down. It didn't matter. It was just a matter of curiosity.

Sam kicked him, and he lifted his gaze. "What?"

"Where did you go?"

"Right here." He brushed off her question. Actually, he'd been thinking of maybe asking Sam on a proper date. He'd been thinking about it a lot. He was attracted to her, and God knew he was over Allison. She'd made it plain she would never be interested in him, and he'd filed that relationship under dead and buried. The only problem with asking Sam out was that it could ruin their working relationship, and he didn't want to do that. Hell, it wasn't the only problem. The biggest problem was that he'd mess it up. His other relationships were disasters. He was too possessive according to one and didn't show enough emotion according to the other. He had absolutely no idea why either said what they had, but no one had ever said he was a ladies' man. He wished people would just talk in plain English sometimes.

As if thinking about Allison had summoned her, the door opened, and she walked in carrying a cake box. She made her way to the table. "Here you go, Samantha. I put 'Happy Birthday, Daddy' on it as you asked."

"Thank you, Allison. I'm sure Mr. Johnson will be happy." Sam smiled at her.

"Are you going out to the Johnsons?" Corrie asked as she walked by, overhearing the conversation between Sam and Allison.

"We are," Ken confirmed.

"I'm going to fix up a birthday meal for them. I know Gen won't mind. Allison, do you have any fresh bread?"

Allison smiled. "I do. And I can put some ice cream in a bag, too. For the cake."

"Candles, too," Edna said. "Say, maybe we can pull together a small gift for him. He hasn't been to town in eons."

"I haven't seen Lawrence in a long time," Corrie added.

"He was having problems with his milk cow last night." Sam threw that bomb into the mix.

Doc Macy, the vet, turned to look at her. "I didn't get a call."

Sam shrugged. "I just know what the kids told us."

Ken heard the murmurs and leaned in toward

Sam. "You realize the entire town will end up on that farm tonight."

Sam dangled her fork from her fingers. "You realize that maybe that's exactly what this guy needs? It has to suck losing the one you love."

Allison snorted. "Save those kinds of comments. Ken wouldn't understand them." The woman tapped the back of Sam's seat. "I'll be back with a few things. Don't leave till I come back."

"Not unless I get called out," Sam agreed. When Allison left, Sam turned slowly toward him and raised both eyebrows. "Explain that."

"Gladly, but not here." Ken took a bite of his lunch. He wished like hell Allison would stop playing the victim. It was a role he'd let her take on, but unfortunately, it seemed to be her entire personality now. Well, at least whenever he was around. And he'd been eighteen when it'd happened, for God's sake. He was an idiot. He'd admitted it.

"Does Garth have call this weekend?" Sam asked, referring to one of the part-time deputies who worked in Bridger County. The sheriff's department had expanded, thanks to a grant from the federal government. The tax base in the county depended on the larger ranches; the smaller ranchers and businesses in Hollister weren't exactly rich. They now had a full-time and a part-time deputy sheriff in the southern part of the county and the same manning the northern part. The sheriff, of course, roamed at his will but wasn't generally doing the political thing until it came time for election, and then, he was hand-holding, baby-kissing, and back-slapping the constituents.

"Yep," he answered. "Why?"

"Thought you'd like to go to the gun range with me. I have a new toy."

Ken put down his fork and blinked at her. They'd never hung out together outside of work. But then again, they lived in separate towns. He wiped his mouth and leaned back. Dare he ask her to his place? Would she take it wrong? Would it be too forward? Was he overthinking it? Probably. "I set up a gun range at my place. What did you get?"

Sam rolled her eyes. "You'll think I'm insane."

Ken moved his fingers across his chest. "Cross my heart, I won't."

"I got a Desert Eagle."

Ken blinked and then whistled. "That's one hell of a lot of gun."

"Right? My dad knew a guy who was selling it.

He mentioned it when we were talking last week. I may have bought it because it's gold plated."

Ken's jaw dropped. "Say what now?"

Sam laughed. "See, I told you."

"No, no, no. I don't think you're insane. Yet. Did you say *gold* plated?"

"Not entirely. It's beautiful. A real work of art." She shrugged. "I'll probably display it and never fire it again, but you know I have to do it at least once."

"I totally get that. I have an old muzzleloader from the Civil War era. My dad tracked down the heritage of the thing through pictures and letters and such. We learned how to load and fire it. And now, it's hanging above my fireplace. I couldn't bring myself to use it again, but I clean it and keep it in working order."

"So, are you a collector?" Sam asked as she pushed her beets away from her potatoes.

"After a fashion. Don't like beets?"

She grimaced. "God, no."

Ken laughed and stabbed one from her plate, popping it into his mouth. He hadn't met a vegetable he didn't love.

"Gross. We can't be friends now." Sam shivered in disgust.

"Oh, damn." He sighed. "Sorry about that, and I thought we had such a good start."

"So did I." She waved at the beets on her plate. "Okay, we can stay friends, just … never eat them in my presence again."

Ken squinted and looked at her. "I can't promise never. I'll try to remember, but you'll have to remind me."

"Deal," Sam agreed.

By the time they'd finished eating, they had dinner, cake, ice cream, a card signed by everyone in the diner, and someone had put a brand-new jackknife into a gift bag for Lawrence. Doc Macy dropped his card in the bag. On the back, he'd put, *Good for one free call out. Happy Birthday.*

"Are you ready to go?" Sam asked him as she stood up.

"I am. Let's get this party started." Ken helped gather all the goods, and they split the load between their cars.

"I'll follow you." Sam slid into her car and started it up.

Ken took off his cowboy hat and got into the driver's seat before heading out of town feeling pretty damn proud of his little corner of the world.

CHAPTER 2

Ken led the way down the gravel road to the farmhouse, where they both parked in front. Craig came out of the house with Buck, followed by Hailey holding the hand of a man Sam hadn't seen before. He wore jeans and a black t-shirt, and his boots were well-worn as he stepped out onto the porch.

"Ken. Is there a problem?" the man asked.

"Hey, Lawrence. Yeah, a small one, but we have something for you first." Ken opened the back door of his vehicle, and Sam moved up to help him with the load from town.

"What's this?" Lawrence asked as Sam put the cake box into his hands.

"Craig and Hailey's birthday present to you."

She slipped the card in her hand behind her back and waved it. She felt Craig take it from her and smiled. "Chocolate, with chocolate frosting."

Hailey smiled and clapped. "Thank you."

"A birthday cake?" Lawrence seemed stunned. "How ... Did they call you?" His eyes shot from the cake to Ken and then to Sam. "I'm sorry, I'm Lawrence Johnson. I don't think we've met."

"Samantha Quinn. I took over for Troy Flores when he retired last year." Sam shook his hand after Lawrence gave Hailey the cake to hold.

"Pleasure," Lawrence said, putting his hand on Hailey's head. He turned to Ken again. "How did this happen?"

"Well, that's the small problem we need to discuss," Ken said. "Craig, Hailey, and Buck took the tractor and headed into Hollister to buy you a cake."

"And a card. We saved our allowances," Hailey added.

"*What?*" Lawrence's shock rolled off him. "You took the tractor on the highway?"

Craig looked down but nodded. Lawrence dropped to his knees in front of his boy. "Craig, you could have been killed if someone were flying over those roads. You know better."

"But you needed a cake," the boy said in a small voice. His eyes were brimming with tears.

"Son, I need you and Hailey more than I need anything else in the world. I can't lose you, too. You are everything to me. Promise me you'll never do that again. Never."

"I promise," Craig sobbed, and Lawrence pulled him into a hug. Sam took the cake from Hailey, and Lawrence pulled his daughter into the embrace. There were mumbled apologies and nothing but unadulterated love between them. The scene before her would make even the hardest of hearts melt. She helped Ken carry the food and cake into the house along with the gift bag. They were invited to stay for cake but excused themselves with the "on duty" response.

As they walked out to their vehicles, Ken nudged her with his elbow. "Feel like running radar?"

That was code for meeting him at their spot. She nodded. "I'm sure we'll be busy. All the traffic going on out here."

"Probably." He smiled and winked at her. Sam did a double take. Please, God, let him be flirting. She didn't know how to be any more obvious that she was interested in him. He was either clueless, clinically dead, or gay to not have caught the hints she was throwing him. She'd watched his lungs expand, so he wasn't dead, and the tension between him and Allison led her to believe he wasn't gay, so clueless had to be the winner. She drove out to the median, where they parked. She faced south, and he faced north, so they could talk while running radar. It was so nice outside that she got out and stood beside her car. There'd been many days that past winter when it was so cold that they'd shared a vehicle and visited, but, when possible, they kept to their units in case they had to respond.

He rolled down his window and pulled out his radar unit. It was older, but he calibrated it with his tuning forks and set it up before she leaned back on her car and asked, "Tell me what's up with you and Allison."

Ken rolled his eyes and puffed his cheeks out before releasing an exasperated sigh. "When you were young, did you ever make a stupid mistake?"

Sam's laugh was automatic. "Holy smokes, yes. Teenage Sam was stupid with a capital S."

"Yeah, well, Allison and I dated in high school. After we graduated, I visited a couple of colleges. I met a girl."

Sam leaned forward. "And …"

"And I liked her, but I didn't tell her about Allison or Allison about her." Ken shrugged. "I was stupid."

"Hell yes, you were." Sam laughed. "How bad was the explosion?"

"Well, you saw Allison today."

"Wait a damn minute." Sam stood up and pointed toward Hollister. "All that today was because you screwed another girl just after high school?"

Ken shook his head. "I didn't sleep with the other girl. She called my house one day when Allison was there."

Sam blinked, trying to wrap her mind around Allison. "So, because you were talking to another woman."

"I kissed her," Ken admitted.

"Wow, that's pretty vile, there, dude. How dare you kiss a girl?" Sam couldn't hold back the laughter. "Please, for the love of God, tell me you're over Allison."

Ken chuckled. "Believe it or not, after college and the sheriff's academy, I followed her around like a love-sick puppy."

Sam stopped laughing. "Why?"

"Because of something my mom told me before she passed. She told me Allison was probably my one shot at happiness. That sat hard." Ken pointed to his brain. "Here." He glanced at her. "But yes. I'm over her." He shrugged. "I've grown up and learned what a true man is and isn't. I'm ashamed of what I did. I've apologized to Allison and the other girl."

"Where's the other girl?"

"I have no idea. She said it wasn't a big deal and that she forgave me, but don't call her again. I didn't." Ken shook his head.

"You've dated since then, right?" Sam leaned against his truck. "A man like you?"

Ken blinked and frowned. "What do you mean a man like me?"

Sam cocked her head. "Sexy? Handsome? Fun? Intelligent? Caring? Can I stop now, or are you fishing for more compliments?" She watched as he turned crimson red, and her jaw dropped. "You don't know how sexy you are, do you?"

Suddenly, he seemed to find the steering wheel interesting and didn't look at her when he answered, "I'm not."

"I beg to differ." Sam shook her head. "Did Allison do this to your ego?"

"Her and some others." Ken shrugged. "I know what I am and what I'm not."

"Do you?" Leaning her hip against his SUV, she stared at him and shook her head. "I don't think so."

"I appreciate the pep talk, but—"

"Pep talk? Yes, yes, you are clueless." Sam threw her hands up into the air. "Hello, Ken? *I* am attracted to *you*. I've dropped every kind of clue I can think of. What does Allison or those other women have that I don't? I'm at a loss here."

His eyes nearly bulged out of their sockets. "What?"

"What, what?" Sam put her hands on her hips. "If you aren't interested, just tell me."

"No!"

Sam laughed. Well, no wonder he didn't catch the clues she was tossing him. He wasn't interested. "Great. Well, okay. I'll be seeing you." She reached for her door handle, but Ken was out of his SUV and putting his hand over hers a second later.

"No, I *am* interested in you. God, I've wanted to ask you out for months."

They were inches apart. Sam only had to look up a bit to look into his eyes, which were a mix of gold and green and rimmed with dark blue. He shifted his hand off hers and moved away. She was tall for a woman, but he was taller and broad through the shoulders. The muscles she could see were promising. *So very promising.* "Then why haven't you asked me out?"

He looked down. "What if it doesn't work out?"

She closed the gap between them. "What if it does?" They were as close as their Kevlar would allow. "Why don't we see where things go? The worst thing that could happen is that we don't have a spark."

Ken wrapped his arm around her waist and shook his head. "There *is* a spark." He dropped his lips to hers, and she made the same sound she'd made earlier when the roast beef hit her tongue. Her body tingled when his lips touched hers. When he licked her lips and invaded her mouth, the tingles morphed into a shockwave that flowed through her body. Feeling the strength in those big arms around her was heaven on earth. She felt positively dainty and feminine in his arms. God, yes, there was a spark. No, check that. A flame-thrower ignited between them.

"K29, status."

She jerked at the sound of her radio from the

patrol car. It should have been coming from her ... She glanced down. Both of their mics were keyed.

They jumped apart and unkeyed the mics of their hand-held radios. She keyed her mic again. "K29 secure."

"Affirm," the dispatcher said. "We have a stranded motorist at mile marker ..."

Sam listened to the call out and acknowledged it. When she was done, she put her hand on Ken's chest. "This, between us, it's good, and I think you're sexy as fuck, Deputy Zorn. Don't let anyone tell you you're not."

She got in and pulled out of the median, heading north to her call. A smile split her lips as she glanced back and saw him standing there, watching her drive away. Clueless, perhaps, but man, that deputy was sexy as hell.

CHAPTER 3

Ken woke up early. He was accustomed to working from dawn to dusk. He clocked eight hours, but for the past fifteen years, it seemed like he was always on duty. His overtime would take a hit now that the department had hired more help, providing him weekend coverage, but the work-life balance was amazing. He wasn't aware of how much he needed the actual downtime. Not having call was liberating and a bit unsettling. Bridger County didn't have enough deputies for around the clock coverage, so even when Ken was home, he was still on call. He wasn't sure what he would do with actual time off. It had been so long.

He'd been a deputy for fifteen years. Damn. He

shook his head and sipped his coffee as he sat outside on his porch, watching the sunrise. He'd been promoted to senior deputy last year. Not that anyone around there knew it. But he'd taken on administrative duties like scheduling and training. He'd convinced the sheriff to apply for the grants and funds to help hire the part-time coverage.

Ken smiled wryly. Of course, the county commissioners, Andrew Hollister Senior, and Frank Marshall, may have known the funds were available and forced the sheriff's agreement on the issue. Colby Reicher was a hands-off type of sheriff, to the point that some in the county were questioning what he actually did. Ken took a drink of his coffee. It was a good question. He couldn't answer it, and while he wasn't accountable to the county's people like Colby, Ken made sure he made the rounds and knew the people who lived in his area. It was country life, and that was what he knew.

The sound of a motor coming down the drive pulled his eyes to the road. He was expecting her patrol car, not the older model SUV that bounced down the gravel road. Sam parked next to his patrol vehicle and got out, carrying a gun case with her. Not that he was looking at the gun case.

He was staring at the woman. Her deep auburn hair reached the middle of her back. She was stunning without the Kevlar vest and the bulk of her gun belt. Slim and fit, Sam wore jeans that hugged her curves and an old t-shirt that snugged up in all the right places. Damn, she was beautiful.

"Good morning. Where's my coffee?" Sam asked as she stepped up onto the porch.

"In the kitchen." Ken opened the door for her.

Sam glanced around his living room. "Oh, nice."

He wasn't the type to keep shit around just for the hell of it, so he didn't keep it if it didn't have a purpose. His furnishings were minimal. "I'm not an interior decorator, that's for sure."

"No, really, I like that it isn't cluttered. I get itchy when stuff is stacked on top of stuff. My mom has all these knickknacks and bobbles that have kind of taken over the front room. My apartment is not like that, I guarantee you." Sam followed him into the kitchen, where he pulled down a big yellow mug and poured her a cup of coffee.

"The creamer is in the fridge. Sugar is on the table." He pulled out a spoon for her and set it on a napkin, then glanced at the case she'd placed on the tabletop. "Is that it?" Ken asked as she added creamer to her coffee.

"It is." Sam's eyes sparkled. "Open it. I want to see what you think."

Ken pulled out the chair and sat down. He unclasped the fasteners and lifted the lid. Blowing out a long whistle, he picked up the weapon. He'd seen movies with the heroes firing these guns, but he'd never held one. He pulled back the slide out of habit to ensure the chamber was clear before examining the gun's artistry. The weapon was a high gloss chrome that someone had affixed gold scrolled plating to along the barrel, the grip, and the upper receiver. The result was beauty rather than function, but damn … "I can see why you bought it."

Sam sat down with her coffee and added a teaspoon of sugar. "My dad thought it was a waste of money."

Ken shook his head. "If you have the money and want it, I don't see a problem buying it." He lifted the gun and got a good sight picture. "She's heavy."

"I know, and that's without the magazine." Sam took a sip of her coffee. "Ah, nirvana."

Ken chuckled. "Thanks. We can take her out

when we finish our coffee. Did you bring anything else to fire?"

"I was hoping you'd ask. I have two new shotguns I need to zero in. I have my turkey license."

Ken's head snapped in her direction. "You hunt?"

She nodded. "God, yes. My dad and I apply for elk every year, but we've never been lucky enough to win that lottery. We've hunted deer, antelope, goose, and duck. Mom and I can cook just about any kind of game you can imagine. Of course, in the fall, I have to go back to the eastern side of the state and get my quota of pheasant."

"Why go back? We've got good pheasant hunting on this side of the state." Ken had harvested his fair share of the bird. They were good eating.

"Ah, my dad is friends with one of the biggest corn farmers on the west side of the Missouri River. Come with me this year, and I'll show you what a multitude of pheasants looks like." She took another sip of her coffee. "Usually, when I tell a guy I like to hunt, I get funny looks."

"Not from men around here. Hunting is a way to put meat in the freezer. I always apply for my licenses, too. Now that I have some free time, I hope to enjoy hunting again. Have you ever gone after wild turkey?"

She squinted her eyes, staring at him. "You don't mean the whiskey, do you?"

Ken laughed. "No, I don't."

"I haven't, but I've been doing some research. Cagey critters?"

"Not necessarily. My dad had a principle with turkeys: Go early and stay late. If you scout out the territory, it makes things easier. Know where they roost and forage. We staked out two or three decoys to attract the males that were old and roosting together or the occasional Tom that was aggressive and combative, especially in the spring. We'd find the high ground, stake our turkeys, and take turns watching. On other days, we'd run and gun. Depended on what Dad was feeling like."

"Did you get your license this year?"

"I did," Ken admitted.

"Go hunting with me? Show me how to find where they roost and feed?"

"Are you asking me on a date, Trooper Quinn?"

"Absolutely." She smiled at him over her coffee cup. "I'm excited to have someone to go hunting with."

"So am I. Speaking of hunting, do you ever

bow hunt?" Ken loved to bow hunt. It took some of the modern advantages away from the equation.

Sam's eyes popped open. "I've never had the opportunity. Would you teach me?"

"I can try." Ken nodded. "We'd have to get you a bow."

"Oh, no problem. Just tell me what I need." She set her cup down. "I feel like a kid in a candy shop. I'm so excited."

Ken smiled at her. The flush that flooded her cheeks and the happiness that radiated from her was something he quite enjoyed. The other relationships he had were all about him trying to please the women he was with, never about them enjoying their time with him. Which should have told him something, but no one had ever said he was a Casanova. Yep, he liked seeing Sam happy. It made him feel like he'd actually done something right. "We'll have to make an appointment at the archery range down south. You'll need to shoot through an array of bows to find out which one feels right for you. I have a compound bow and a recurve. I use the compound bow for hunting whitetail, and the recurve, which was handmade, sits in the corner of the front room."

"Oh, by the old muzzleloader?" Sam jumped up and went back into the living room. "Where is it?"

Ken stood up and leaned against the door of the kitchen, pointing down the hall. "Above my fireplace. Last door on the right."

He'd added a primary suite to the house about five years ago. The room was almost the size of the rest of his house. "Wow." Samantha glanced back at him, standing in the doorway. "Where the heck did this come from?" she said as she stepped into the bedroom. Ken meandered after her. There was a sitting room with a television on a low built-in credenza. Past the sitting area, centered between it and the bedroom, was a double-sided fireplace made of local Fairburn agate.

"This is amazing." Samantha spun and then looked up. "Exposed beams!" She turned back to him. "Did you do this?"

"Most of it. I called in friends when I needed help. Tegan ran the electrical, and I had it plumbed by a guy down in Belle." He was pretty proud of the addition.

"How long did it take you?"

"About three years to complete, but I did it without going into debt."

"You did the flooring?" She looked down at the

dark wood planks.

"I did."

"You're amazing." She smiled, and her eyes landed on the muzzleloader. "Man, that is a long-ass rifle."

"Right?" Ken entered the bedroom and set his coffee cup on the fireplace mantel. He took the gun down and handed it to her. She held it reverently, the same way he'd handled her gold-plated pistol. Respecting weapons was the first order of safety.

"So, this is where you put the powder?"

Ken lowered the holding area as she held it and nodded. "Quad F powder, but you do that only after you've loaded the bullet." He took an old oak box from the mantel. "These are the bullets. Over here are the wads that go around them as you move them down and seat them at the end. Usually, these are oiled, but I didn't want to store them that way."

"Too true. Fire hazard, anyone?" Sam laughed.

"Absolutely. Then, after you take out the ramrod you used to seat the bullet gently but firmly, you turn the weapon like this. Put the powder in here. The powder needs to make it to this small chamber here. Then you cock the weapon. When the flint comes forward, it ignites the powder, and the bullet is expelled."

She nodded. "Kentucky windage. Do you realize how much you'd have to fire this weapon to be even remotely proficient?"

"Yeah, I've often thought about that. Do you think that's why they lined up in a row during the Revolutionary War?" Ken shook his head. "Stupid assumption on my part."

"Not really," she said. "The chances of this being loaded with the exact powder to reach the adversary are probably pretty low. Do you know what the average range is?"

"I don't. As I said, we only shot it once." As he responded, she handed the gun back to him.

"That is a piece of history. You know I'm going to have to research muzzleloaders now."

Ken returned the weapon to the display hooks installed on the mantel. "I could think of worse things to research."

"Like UFOs?" Sam's throaty laugh bounced around the room.

Ken dropped his head back and looked up at the ceiling. "I'm just glad she's off the Bigfoot trail."

"She's not," Sam said as she walked past the fireplace. "You have floor-to-ceiling windows."

"What do you mean she's not? And yeah, I love the view." He walked up behind her. Her perfume, or shampoo, or hell, toothpaste, whatever the smell was, made its way to him, and instantly, he had images of her naked on his king-sized bed.

"She was talking about the Bigfoot. She said she had a picture."

"When was this?" Ken asked.

"When I was at Allison's to buy the birthday cake. She was telling … I'm not sure who the guy was, but she told him she couldn't talk about it because she didn't want a bunch of people to show up and start looking for him."

"Oh, for fuck's sake." Ken rubbed his neck and glanced at her. "Sorry for the language."

"Yeah, I'm totally offended." Sam crossed her eyes at him. "Not."

"Can you describe who she was talking to?"

"I haven't seen him before. He was a tall man, six foot four or five, maybe. Broad through the shoulders, square chin. American Indian. His hair was down to the middle of his back. I'm envious of how straight it was."

"Did he have a white straw cowboy hat with a black and silver band?"

She nodded. "Yep. That's him."

"Mike White Cloud. Thank God. I'll leave it to him to tell Mr. Marshall that Edna is at it again."

Sam put her hands on her hips. "Why? *Is* there a Bigfoot in the area?"

Ken laughed. "Nah, and there aren't any UFOs either."

"Are you sure about that? Area 51 is real." Sam crossed her arms and stared at him.

"The location is real. The aliens aren't." Ken lifted an eyebrow. "Do I need to worry?"

Sam lost control of her stern face and smiled. "Nope. But I want to go to Loch Ness and see Nessie." She waved at the windows. "Don't you feel slightly exposed with all this and no curtains?"

Ken shook his head. He walked to the bed and picked up a remote. Pointing it at one panel, he pushed the down arrow, and a shade rolled down from the top of the window. "It's between the panes of glass." Sam marveled at the device the same way he had. The first thing he'd bought when he decided to add to the house were those windows. He'd seen them online and then went to Denver to see them in person. They were expensive but worth every penny. Ken put the remote down. "Are you ready to go play with your new toy?"

"Absolutely."

* * *

SAM WAS RIDICULOUSLY HAPPY. Ken, off duty, was everything she'd imagined he'd be. And Heavens above, the man's body. Strong shoulders and arms that stretched the fabric of his t-shirt were instantaneously visible. She could go on for hours about the way his chest filled out his shirt or the way his body narrowed at the waist, and then those thighs. Delicious. Ken Zorn in a uniform was yummy. Ken Zorn in tight jeans … She'd about swallowed her tongue when she walked up those steps. He affected her in ways no one else ever had, and while it was a little scary, she liked the electric feeling that zapped through her whenever they were together. Sam had had several relationships, but inevitably, it seemed like she was the alpha in the relationship, and that was something she didn't want. She wanted a man to protect her, even though she could kick ass. She wanted a man to treat her like a lady even after she outshot him. She needed her man to be secure enough in his manhood to be the alpha in the relationship, not just simply fade away into the background. Was she a larger-than-life personality? Yes, and that was her biggest problem when it came to relationships. Either the men wanted to compete with her, or they disappeared. She didn't want to compete. She wanted to feel safe, loved, and secure enough to be herself with the guy she was with. She'd never found someone like that before.

After gathering their weapons and ammo, she followed him past the huge garage to the back of his property.

"You made a berm?" The mound of earth was easily twenty feet tall.

Ken opened a small shed and reached in, pulling out silhouette targets. "It was the responsible thing to do. Kinzer's dairy is about five miles that way. If one of their cows ever decided to be a renegade…"

"You love this community, don't you?"

He handed her the targets and grabbed a staple gun from inside the shed. "I once thought I'd move away and never come back."

"After Allison broke up with you?"

Ken made a noise in the back of his throat. "Stupid is as stupid does. Come on." They set their weapons and ammo down at the firing line and walked down the shooting range to hang the targets. "Yeah, it was about that time when I decided this wasn't the place for me. But after I finished my associate's degree, I saw an opportunity to attend the sheriff's academy. I'm not the best student, so I thought, why not? I was placed right back here. Obviously, someone had a plan for me."

"I get that," Sam said as she held the target to the wooden frame, and Ken stapled it on. "I finished college and law school. My parents wanted me to be a lawyer. Dad never wanted me to become a trooper."

"The enforcement side of the law attracted you?" Ken asked as they moved to the other target.

"Yeah, my dad is in law enforcement. I grew up around it."

"Really? Is he still working?"

Samantha snorted. "Reid Quinn, Superintendent of the South Dakota Highway Patrol."

Ken stopped with the staple gun and turned to face her. "Your father?"

"Yep." It was her turn to roll her eyes.

"How in the hell did you wind up with Hollister as your patrol area? You could be anywhere. Aberdeen, Brookings, Sioux Falls, Rapid..."

"I was in Pierre, right under Dad's nose. I hated

it. When I saw that Troy Flores was retiring, I jumped on the opportunity to be my own woman instead of the superintendent's daughter."

Ken's mouth ticked up in a smile. "That's noble. I'm not sure I'd be so willing to leave a choice patrol sector."

Sam narrowed her eyes at him. "That's bullshit."

Ken snorted. "Yeah, it is. I'm kind of proud of you for making your own way. You're a hell of a cop, from what I've seen."

"Well, thank you. Right back at you. You're engrained in this community."

Ken hit the bottom of the target with a staple. "Seem to be, that's true," he agreed as they walked back to the firing line. "So, a law school graduate. That's impressive. Do you think you'll ever practice?"

Sam sighed. "Maybe. I love what I'm doing, but as I get older … I don't know. I have options, thanks to my dad. I think I would have enjoyed a general law practice. Not family law. I think seeing all those divorces would suck the life out of me. Criminal defense wouldn't be my choice either."

"True. Those two areas get a lot of crap dumped on them. Let's load your museum piece and see what she can do."

Sam pulled out the loaded magazine and inserted it. Before she chambered a round, she removed her earplugs from the pouch dangling from her neck. She put on her shooting glasses and earplugs. Then she glanced over at Ken, who had his earplugs and range glasses on. "Ready?"

He nodded. "Let her rip."

Sam squared up on her target and lifted her pistol. It was too heavy for her to hold with a single hand. She supported herself with her opposite hand under the grip, then flipped the lever, put the weapon on fire, and lined up her sight picture.

Slowly, she squeezed the trigger. The kick of the weapon was beyond anything she'd ever experienced. The weapon's muzzle lifted nearly straight up. "Holy cow!" Sam pointed the weapon toward the ground. "Holy cow," she said again. Her hands were shaking. She'd almost lost her grip on the damn thing.

"Hell of a kick," Ken said.

"Yeah, once is enough." She wouldn't be a statistic. That gun and her lack of upper body strength was an accident waiting to happen.

"Here." Ken moved behind her and lifted her arm back up. He gripped her arm and lowered his mouth to her ear. "Line it up. I've got you." Still shaking, but not sure if it was from the weapon's kick or the closeness of the man behind her, she lifted the weapon to line up her sight picture. "Whenever you're ready," Ken spoke softly.

She squeezed the trigger. His body behind her and his grip on her arm steadied her, so the kick, while still extreme, didn't scare her.

Ken's chin landed on her shoulder. "You're pulling to the right."

Sam blinked, trying hard to decipher what he was saying. His scent had enveloped her, and the thrill of having him so close muddled her thoughts. She blew out a breath and looked down range. The two holes on the target were indeed to the right of center. "Do you have a sight tool?"

"I do." Ken moved away from her and headed back to the small shed.

"Damn, girl, get a grip." She flipped the weapon to safe and sat on the ammo can she'd brought.

"Here."

She inserted the small, slotted tool into the sight and clicked it twice to move the center of her shot to the right. "I'd go three," Ken said as he looked at the target.

She glanced down range and stared at the holes. "Agreed." She clicked the screw again and handed Ken back the tool. She stood, and he took his place behind her again. Knowing she had his support, she fired and nailed the bullseye dead center.

"Excellent shot. Do it again."

She emptied the clip, making a hell of a hole in the center of the target. "Your turn." She released the clip, shoved it into her back pocket, and loaded a fresh clip for him.

"Are you sure?" he asked before taking the weapon.

"Absolutely. You got to feel the power of this thing. Just watch out; she's a mule."

Ken smiled, winked at her, and assumed his stance in front of the other target. He fired, and the weapon kicked.

"Damn." Ken moved his feet farther apart and fired again. A smile spread across his face, and he emptied the magazine. "I think I might have to get me one of these," he said as he handed her the empty and safe weapon.

"Right? What a rush," she agreed and put the weapon inside the case. When she stood up, Ken was right beside her.

"What a rush." His hand cupped around her neck, and he pulled her into him. As his lips found hers, she melted into him. That electrical feeling zapped a shiver down her spine and curled her toes. That never before felt flamethrower blazed a hot path to her core. She clung to him and soaked in the sensation of rightness. He wasn't competing with her; he was leading her. He wasn't blending into the background; he was standing beside her. He was everything she'd ever wanted and never found.

When he pulled away, she opened her eyes and gazed at him. "Hell of a kick, huh?"

Ken smiled. "Hell of a kick. We should probably finish what we're doing here."

Sam licked her lips and watched as his eyes followed her gesture. "If we finish what we're doing here, we'll never sight in my shotguns."

His laughter filled the air. "True. That is so very true. Let's table this portion for later."

"Deal," she agreed as he bent down for another kiss. It was short but full of promise. Sam sighed in contentment and leaned against him when he stopped the kiss.

"Are you okay?" His hand rubbed up and down her back. Possessive and protective.

Sam smiled and lifted. "Better than I've been in a long, long time."

* * *

SEVEN BOXES OF AMMUNITION LATER, they both walked away from his gun range with smiles. Their hearing protection hung from their necks, and both had their shooting glasses tipped back on top of their heads. "The twelve gauge is probably the one I'm going to go with for turkey season."

"You had a great grouping with that at forty yards," Ken agreed. "And your Eagle would drop an elephant."

"Yep, not hunting elephants or anything safari-type. I prefer to eat what I kill, not stuff and mount them."

"Too true. Killing just to kill is pointless. Some families around here survive off game."

"I haven't met the game warden yet." Sam stopped and turned to him. "You do have a game warden up here, right?"

"Sure, but you won't see him much. Out-of-state season is when he's run ragged."

"I can only imagine. During pheasant season, we'd get private planes landing and hunting parties, already drunk, unloading to go out. Scary times."

"Ever hear the one about the mule deer?" Ken

asked as they walked to the small shed he'd built to hold his weapon-cleaning products. They laid down their weapons and found the rods, bore brushes, and cleaning swabs that would work for their weapons.

"No. Is this a stupid crime story?" Sam asked as she disassembled her Desert Eagle.

"Oh, yeah." Ken broke down his service revolver. He'd plunked a box of ammo down range. Keeping proficient with his weapon could save his life someday. "It was down in the southern part of the state. Some out-of-state people showed up and had tags for mule deer. They took off down past Edgemont, out farther than Provo, to that area near the Nebraska border. Well, when they came back into town that night, they proudly strapped their kill across the hood of their Suburban."

Sam had stopped cleaning her Eagle. "What happened?"

"They'd killed a rancher's mule."

The look of shock on her face was the same one he'd worn when the game warden had told him what had happened. "You've got to be kidding?"

"Nope. That and the stupid guys fired toward the house from the road. The rancher's wife and kids were in that old place—the bullets lodged in the tar paper shingles covering that portion of the house. The rancher called it in after his wife called him. So, they were arrested by the county sheriffs when they came back through Provo, and the game warden issued a slew of citations as well. One of the rancher's kids filmed the SUV from the house window as they opened the pasture gate to go in and load that old Jack onto the hood. Trespassing was added to the counts."

Sam's jaw was slack as she shook her head in disgust. "Please tell me they got jail time."

"Nope. Community service. They had to work for the rancher for thirty days, pay for the mule, and they've been banned from hunting in the state. Rumor has it the judge thought highly of that Jack. Most expensive mule in the country as far as we know."

"Well, that's as it should be. I can't believe how irresponsible some people are when they carry deadly weapons." She stopped what she was doing. "You're not pulling my leg about this, are you?"

Ken lifted his right hand. "Swear it's the truth. The game warden who wrote the citations told me."

"Absolutely insane." Sam snorted. "What time is it?"

Ken glanced at his watch. "Damn, nearly eleven. Let's take care of these, then grab lunch at the diner."

"Okay, but I'm cooking dinner for you." Sam glanced up. "If you'll let me use your kitchen."

Ken would let her use whatever the hell she wanted. "Any time. What are you making?"

"Not beets." Sam made a face at him.

"You really don't like those, do you?"

"No. Slimy things."

"They aren't slimy."

"They totally are," Sam argued. "Now, hurry up, I'm hungry."

Ken laughed as they cleaned their weapons. The tedious work flew by as they visited and swapped stories. To say he enjoyed the time would be an understatement. There weren't many pauses in their conversations, and those that happened were natural and comfortable. He understood what she was saying, and more still, he understood the unsaid facts that most people would typically have to have explained. They spoke the same language when they visited and shared details of their lives. Sam was sharing one as they locked up the shed, making sure to police all their brass and shells.

"You're joking," Ken said.

"I'm not. It was the worst fatality accident I've ever investigated. Semi versus motorcycle. The force of the collision decapitated the motorcyclist, but the helmet stayed where it was supposed to. We found his head and the helmet about twenty-five feet away." Sam shivered. "That's why I'll never ride a motorcycle."

Ken grabbed her shotgun and then took her free hand in his. "I probably would have nightmares about something like that." He wasn't afraid to admit that the fatality accidents he'd worked on haunted him.

"I still do, occasionally. It was my first and worst fatality." Sam sighed. "That sounded bad, they're all horrible."

Ken squeezed her hand. "I know what you mean. Some are just more gruesome than others."

"They are." She squeezed his hand back. "It's amazing to talk to someone who understands. Someone who gets it."

He nodded. "I agree. It's special." They walked for a while before he asked, "Do you want to put these in the house or your SUV?"

"The house is fine. Are we taking your patrol vehicle?" She entered the house and set the case holding her Desert Eagle on the floor by the couch.

"Yep. One of the perks of being a senior deputy. I can use it full-time."

"I need to wash up." Sam held up her hands. "Gun oil."

"First door on your right," Ken said and watched her go down the hall. The sway of her hips was not missed. He went into the kitchen and washed up.

She joined him a few minutes later. "You mentioned food?"

"I did." He grabbed his keys off the ring by the kitchen door. "I'm buying." Ken stipulated that upfront. Sam had been adamant about paying for her lunches or breakfasts when they'd eaten in uniform. Well, until yesterday.

"Deal, but I'm buying the groceries for dinner." Sam walked past him and brushed against him, even though there was more than enough room. He followed her out the door and locked the house. He didn't leave his home open unless he was on the property.

They pulled into the diner and went inside. Corrie greeted them as she buzzed by with a tray full of specials. Ken made eye contact with everyone and shook Andrew Hollister's hand. He and Gen usually made an appearance on the weekend. She'd take inventory and order things that the diner needed. Corrie and Ciera ran the business for the most part now that Gen was pregnant. What they said about women glowing with happiness when pregnant was true. He'd seen it in Hollister, and he believed it. Kids were a blessing.

"Hi, Sam," Gen said. "What are you two up to today?"

"We've been firing weapons all morning. Ken helped me zero them in, and then we just plunked slugs down range for a while. It was fun."

Ken dropped his arm over Sam's shoulder. The act sent Gen's eyebrows heavenward before a huge smile split her lips. "You'll have to excuse me, but I'm not sure I'd classify that as fun."

"Have you ever shot a gun?" Sam asked.

"Ah, no." Gen shook her head.

"Well, when you aren't in the condition you're in now, I'll take you out to a firing range, or if Ken will let us use his, we won't have to travel as far. I'm telling you; the thrill is something you need to experience."

Gen made a face. "I'll probably pass."

"Your loss." Sam laughed.

"I'll suck it up." Gen laughed with her.

"You two here for the special?" Corrie asked as she passed them on her way to the kitchen.

"Yes," Ken called after her. Once they'd reached their booth, Sam slid in, and Ken slid in beside her.

She looked up at him and smiled. "I like this."

"So do I." Ken bent down and kissed her softly.

"Here are your drinks." Corrie smiled as she set the sodas down. "So happy to see you on one side of the booth. I had a feeling it would turn out this way. Although, I have to admit, I'd thought you'd be quicker about it, Ken."

He felt his face flame, and Sam put her hand on his. "He was worried it might affect our working relationship. It won't." Sam winked at him.

Corrie cocked her head. "I never thought about that. I imagine, as professional as you both are, that if things didn't work out, neither of you would let it into the business of law enforcement."

"Which is one hundred percent true," Sam agreed.

"Good. Well, if you ask me, you're good together. I'll go get your food." She was off before Ken could say a word.

"You realize it'll be all over town now."

Ken snorted. "Well, not as quickly as it would be if Edna and her cronies were here."

"Edna's a nice person. Just a bit too interested in everyone." Sam chuckled.

"That's one way to put it. I've been dealing with her for the last fifteen years. She's harmless, but man, can she spread gossip."

"Faster than Phil?" Sam asked as she took a sip of her drink.

Ken laughed. "Maybe not. Phil is definitely plugged in."

"You grew up here?"

"I did." Ken nodded down the street. "The school houses kindergarten through twelfth grade. We all grew up together." He motioned around the diner. "Sometimes that's a good thing, and sometimes it can be a detriment."

As he spoke, Allison walked into the diner with Kathy Prentiss. Their laughter stopped abruptly when Allison saw him sitting with his arm around Sam's shoulder.

"Ruh-roh, Scooby," Sam whispered as she lifted her drink to her lips.

Ken turned and smiled down at her. "I don't care. I'm happy. I'm with the woman I want to be with. She's ancient history. You're my present and, hopefully, my future."

Sam glanced over at the booth where Kathy and Allison sat down. "Well, if the look I'm getting could kill, I wouldn't be anyone's future."

Ken glanced over in time to see Allison whip her eyes toward the window. He turned back to Sam. "I'm with the person I want to be with. Her looks have no influence or impact on how I feel for you or how little I care about her angst and drama."

"Good." Sam set her drink down as Corrie brought out their lunch, saying, "Homemade tamales, rice, and beans. Here are some corn chips and salsa. Can I get you anything else?"

"No, thanks. I'm starving," Sam said, picking up her fork.

Ken was, too. He could feel the hole that Allison was boring into his back, but it didn't matter. As they ate, he and Sam laughed and talked about stupid excuses that traffic stop people gave them. "I swear. She said, 'But, officer, I was going downhill!' I replied, 'Ma'am, the speed limit is the same going up the hill as it is going down the hill.' She had the audacity to show up in court and tell the judge the same thing."

"Was she insane?" Ken wiped his mouth.

"No. She was serious! She said the speed limit shouldn't apply downhill because of gravity's effect on the heavy vehicle. But get this: She was driving a foreign job that weighed less than our gun belts! The judge listened with a straight face, banged his gavel, pronounced her guilty, and told her that the speed limit was the same going down the hill as it was going up. I didn't prompt him or tell him what I'd said. She glared daggers at me."

Ken didn't see Allison leave or care that she had. When they were done, he paid the bill, and they strolled across the street to the small grocery store. He placed his arm over Sam's shoulder as they walked. He let it drop when they entered the store but took her hand. After grabbing a basket, they walked back to the meat counter.

Mr. Sanderson was behind the display cases, and he smiled when he saw Ken. "Deputy, how's it going?"

"Fine, sir. Samantha wants to get something for dinner tonight."

Sam smiled up at him. "I was hoping for some double-cut pork chops?"

"I can do that for you. I have a slab of chops in the cooler. How many do you want?"

"Three, please. He'll eat two." She nodded to Ken.

"That sounds about right. I'll bring them out when I'm done. You can finish your shopping."

"Who was that?" Sam asked as they wandered down the aisle.

Ken stopped. "Damn, I'm sorry. I didn't know you hadn't met Allison's dad."

"Hi, Ken." The voice from behind them turned both of them. "Mrs. Sanderson." He nodded. "This is Samantha Quinn. She's the state trooper assigned to our area."

"One of them." Sam reached out a hand.

Mrs. Sanderson smiled and shook Sam's hand. "It's wonderful to meet you. You're the one who came in to buy a cake for Lawrence Johnson, right?"

"I am, but it was Ken's idea. Those kids were so sweet." Sam glanced up at him.

"Well, we're all obliged that you both took an interest. Sometimes, life gets hectic, and we forget that others are hurting. Can I help you find anything?"

"I need potatoes, onions, and apples." Turning to Ken, she asked, "Oh, do you have cinnamon?"

"Ah, that would be a no." Ken had two spices.

Salt and pepper. That was why he ate at the diner most days.

"Cinnamon, too." Sam laughed.

"Right this way." Sam followed Mrs. Sanderson as Mr. Sanderson came out with a white paper-wrapped selection of pork chops.

"That's a nice lady." Allison's dad said as Ken took the pork from him.

"She is. I'm sorry I didn't know you hadn't been introduced." Ken apologized for his lack of manners.

"Ah, I knew who she was. Seen her around. Just happy you found someone. Now, if we could get Allison settled, I could relax." Mr. Sanderson elbowed him gently. "Wish me luck."

"Good luck, sir," Ken said, moving toward where Sam and Mrs. Sanderson were selecting potatoes from a bin.

After Sam paid for the food, they moseyed back across the street to his patrol vehicle. Frank Marshall's truck pulled into the free parking space next to his as they got in.

"Sam, have you met Mr. Marshall?"

"I have. I introduced myself a couple of months back." She put her seat belt on.

"Could you give me a minute? There's something I need to talk to him about."

"Sure. Take your time." She rolled down her window as she spoke.

Ken got out and met up with Frank. "Sir, do you have a minute?"

Frank nodded and leaned against the grill of his truck. He reached into his shirt pocket and pulled out two pieces of taffy, handing one to Ken. "Figure I know what you're going to say."

"I heard she was talking to Mike about a Bigfoot picture she took."

"Yup. Mike told me. The thing is, I have the photo, and I have the negative. So, if she's hell-bent on stirring up things, she'd have to ask for the negative back, and, son, I have just plum forgotten what I did with that thing. You know, later in life, your memory starts to go."

"Sir, I doubt you've ever forgotten a thing in your life."

Frank winked at him. "Anything else you need, son?"

"No, sir. Just checking to make sure everything was taken care of." Ken laughed and popped the taffy into his mouth.

"I got something to ask of you. Was going to

wait, but figured you'd need time to chew on the idea for a while."

Ken felt his eyebrows raise. "You know I'll do anything for you, sir. What do you need?"

"You to run for sheriff."

Ken inhaled so sharply that he sucked down the taffy he'd just put in his mouth. He grabbed his neck and felt a massive and mighty whap on his back. The candy flew from his throat to the dirt at his feet.

"Shit, son, didn't mean to kill you," Frank said as Sam raced out of the car.

Ken took several deep breaths, then looked up at Frank. "Sir, you gotta warn a person before you say things like that."

"Are you okay?" Sam slid to a stop by him. He nodded and dropped his arm around her.

"Well, consider it for a minute. We'll talk about it later." Frank tipped his hat at Sam. "Trooper, pleasure." He strolled down the boardwalk and walked into the hardware store.

"What did he say?" Sam asked.

Ken glanced around. "He wants me to run for sheriff."

Sam blinked up at him and then smiled. "I think you should."

CHAPTER 4

Sam sat across from Ken as he shook his head. The topic of his running for sheriff had been the afternoon's focus. "I don't have the money for a campaign." He shook his head. "Colby has the name recognition, and the people in the northern part of the county don't know me."

Sam nodded at his comments. They were basically building a pros and cons list. Ken would get around to realizing running for sheriff was a no-brainer, but until then, she'd support him by listening. "What else?"

"Sorry?" Ken blinked and looked at her.

"What else? I know you've recently completed your bachelor's degree in criminal justice and

KEN

spent fifteen years serving the people of this county. You were the one who wrote the grants and funding requests for the recent budget and manning increase. One of the county commissioners asked you to consider running. That probably means he's talked to others on the board."

"And if I fail to get elected? Man, I'd have to quit because Colby would make my life hell."

Sam tapped her fingers on the table. "What if you were able to find another job? One with a state agency." She bit her bottom lip after she tossed out the question.

Ken's eyes narrowed. "What do you mean?"

"You could work for the State Highway Patrol."

Ken shook his head. "I couldn't go through another academy. Damn, I was fifteen years younger, and the one I went through almost killed me."

Sam put her hand on his. "You wouldn't have to. I know for a fact several officers from different organizations have transferred to the state patrol. They go through the classes about jurisdiction and the other administrative areas, but they aren't required to do any other things. No five-mile runs or thousands of pushups." She smiled at him. "But I think you'd pass the physical aspects with flying colors."

Ken fell back against the chair. "I don't know."

Sam got up and went behind him. She slid her hands onto his shoulders and started to rub.

"Oh, shit. Don't ever stop," Ken groaned in a deep growl.

"How about we table the talk of running for sheriff and do something fun?"

Ken tipped his head back, and she looked down at him. "Like?"

"Do you have cards, a board game?"

"Chess?"

"I love chess. You go find it while I get dinner going."

In the kitchen, she browned the pork chops and put them in the oven to finish cooking. The potatoes she boiled to mash, and the apples and onions plus the cinnamon and a couple of teaspoons of sugar went into a saucepan with some water to cook down. She grabbed some frozen green beans that she'd nuke right before they ate.

Ken came into the kitchen, lifting the case she assumed held the chessboard.

"I can set this up here or in the sitting room."

"Let's play here until dinner is ready, and we can resume after in the sitting room," Sam said as she stirred the applesauce.

"You got it." Ken set the board up. "Would you like to have a drink? I have the usual suspects, but no wine."

"I like everything, not just wine." Sam waved her free hand as she turned the potatoes down a bit so they wouldn't boil over. "What do you have?"

"Whiskey, tequila, vodka, beer, and I think I have bourbon."

Sam stopped and turned around. "Isn't bourbon whiskey?"

"Yep, but not all whiskey is bourbon." Ken shrugged. "A piece of information that has stuck in my brain."

"Right. Okay. Well, vodka and OJ." She'd seen the bottle of juice when putting away the groceries that afternoon.

"Coming right up." After Ken mixed them both a drink, they sat down. "Flip for white?"

"What? You're not going to let your guest be white?" She fanned out her fingers and placed them on her chest, batting her eyes simultaneously.

"I'm going to regret playing you, aren't I?"

"Probably. I was the president of our high school chess club."

Ken chuffed out a laugh. "I thought only geeks played chess in high school."

"I was a total geek."

"Bullshit." Ken laughed and took a sip of his Jack and Coke.

"No, really. I wore braces until my senior year. I got great grades but was *never* in the popular set. My best friend had glasses so thick that her eyes looked like she was looking through a microscope, you know? She got corrective surgery but still wears glasses. They aren't as thick, thankfully. The boys didn't like me any more than the girls did. I was too aggressive and abrupt. I didn't put up with their shit. When I beat up the future star quarterback in the fifth grade, my shot at being popular went down the tubes."

Ken laughed. "You beat up a boy in the fifth grade? Why?"

"Because he said some bad things about my friend. You know, the one with the glasses. Her name is Carol, and she's one of the nicest people in the world. But you know kids, they don't care if you're nice or not, just whether you're like them. She wasn't. I wasn't. So, we were ostracized." She shrugged. "It hurt like hell. I started going to the gym with my dad. He taught me how to box and how to work out. I've always been strong, but he helped funnel my anger. When I'm mad, I work out instead of beating up on future quarterbacks."

Ken laughed. "I was surprised that gun this morning didn't knock you on your ass. I was braced after watching the kickback you received from it, and it was still a shock. You're strong."

She shrugged. "I haven't been as consistent working out as I should be. I can run for miles, but I need to get back to lifting weights. The kick on that gun woke me up to the fact that my upper body strength isn't where it needs to be."

"Then I'll have to join you in the weight room. That Desert Eagle was a monster."

Sam smiled and sat down across from him. She turned the board, so he had the white pieces. "It's a monster, but it sure is pretty. I'll give you white this time."

Ken lifted an eyebrow but smiled at her. "You think you're that good?"

"I know I am. Move, mister," Sam goaded him.

Ken moved his pawn, and Sam settled in. They suspended the match to eat and refill their cocktail glasses. Twice. She felt no pain when they moved the game into the sitting room. Instead of sitting on the chairs, they sat on the floor and faced each other over his low coffee table. Ken lit the fire even though it wasn't needed for heat, but the ambiance was over the top.

She moved and held her finger on her piece, looking for any possible repercussions for the move. Two seconds after withdrawing her finger, she saw what she'd missed. He queenside castled, and she was in checkmate.

Sam flopped down onto the floor. "You beat me!"

Ken appeared above her on his hands and knees. "That'll teach you. Some of us backwoods boys do know a thing or two."

She lifted her hands, grabbed his collar, and pulled him down to her. "Then show me, deputy. Show me what you know."

Sam felt his weight on her as his lips found hers. She wanted it, wanted him in the most agonizing way. His hands slid under her, and he lifted with her to his knees. He broke the kiss, stood up, and walked around the fireplace to the bed. He deposited her in the middle and took off his shirt while staring at her. She stripped off hers. God, he was amazing.

"You're beautiful." His words brought her attention from his chest and arms to his face. She wasn't, but she was comfortable in her skin. She kneed up and unfastened her jeans, shimmying them to her knees, then sat down, extending her legs toward him. He obliged and pulled off the jeans. But Sam wasn't done. She unhooked her bra and dropped it beside her. She laid back, wearing only the white lace boy shorts she'd put on that morning. "Your turn." She lifted her arms and placed them behind her head. Her breasts lifted, and Ken's eyes seemed to run over her a thousand times before he moved. He unhooked his massive belt buckle and then unfastened his jeans. She smiled when she saw the dark blue boxer briefs. So sexy. The impressive bulge in the cotton material let her know she was in for one hell of a night. And that was perfectly fine with her.

He left his boxers on and crawled up the bed. "It's been a long time for me," Ken whispered as he nibbled on the shell of her ear. Her body reverberated with need.

"Been a while for me, too." She didn't sleep around. She had a vibrator and handled the situation if needed, but he ... oh, God, he was perfect. His touch stimulated every nerve ending in her body. She arched under him and spread her legs. He fit between them perfectly. As they kissed and learned about each other's bodies, their hips moved in an ancient dance that she seemed to grasp anew.

She traveled his body with her fingertips and followed the mat of dark brown hair on his chest down his happy trail to the waistband of his briefs. Samantha reached in and circled his cock with her hand. The velvet softness of the hard length was hot and heavy in her hand. The tip was wet, and he was as ready for her as she was for him.

He broke the kiss and stared down at her. "Let me get a condom."

"I've got that covered. As long as you don't give me anything." She stroked his shaft again and watched his eyes roll back into his head.

"Nothing. I'm good." The words were strangled, but she heard them.

"So am I. Get inside me, deputy."

The words seemed to release him. He rose, pulled off her panties, and was out of his briefs in seconds. He came down on top of her, between her legs. She wrapped them around his back, and he slipped his hands under her shoulders and pushed into her core. Both moaning, his head dropped onto her shoulder. "Fuck, so tight."

He retracted and pushed again a bit farther. Her air escaped as he did it again, her words became a whisper on that breath, "So good."

He pushed up on one knee and hilted inside her. She arched under him in absolute bliss. She could feel his cock pulsing inside her. Her body was tight, and she was so close. "So close." The words, her thoughts, were a prayer and a hope. He pulled one hand from behind her and reached down to her clit. In surprise, Samantha's eyes popped open. Ken stared down at her. "I'll get you there, baby. I'll get you there." His finger moved around the tight knot at the apex of her sex, and she writhed under him. He pulled out and moved back in three, four times before she shattered and bucked under him. Her fingers dug into his arms as she felt, for the first time, an orgasm given to her by a man. He raced to his finish, and the sensation of him losing himself inside her almost tripped her over that line again. Her core vibrated with the memory of that orgasm. The realization that he was staring at her came moments later. She opened her eyes. "What?"

"You're the most beautiful woman I've ever seen."

She smiled at him. "Can I tell you a secret?"

He nodded.

"That was the first time a man has made me orgasm."

He blinked and frowned. "What?"

"It's true. I fake it."

He rolled to his right and pulled her with him. She laughed at the sudden movement. He pushed her hair away from her face, but it flopped right back. She laughed again and swiped it to the side. It landed with a huge fall on his chest and face. He laughed, that time pushing her hair out of his face. "I'm sorry the men before me were so greedy."

"I'm not." She leaned down and kissed him. "What I experienced tonight was something special that only you have given me. I'm not sorry about that."

"You make me feel …" He huffed out a breath. "You make me feel like I *am* something special."

"That's because you are, deputy. You truly are. I'll never let you forget that."

"And I'll never let you forget that you are the most beautiful woman, both physically and here, in your heart." He pulled her down for a kiss. "Even if you can't play chess."

Sam laughed and sat up, straddling him. "I demand a rematch without alcohol involved."

"Any time." He sat up and wrapped her in his arms. His cock filled under her.

"Deputy Zorn, do I detect a renewed interest?"

A sexy smile spread across his face. "Trooper Quinn, you should be an investigator. So astute."

She draped her arms over his shoulders. "Perhaps you should show me again how greedy those other men were."

He adjusted her so the tip of his cock was at her core. "We won't ever talk about them again. They don't matter. They don't exist."

She pushed his dark blond hair away from his brow. "And those women who hurt you and made you feel less than special don't matter. They don't exist either."

"Only us." He lifted, his muscles rippling under her hands, and she fell on her back, her head now at the foot of the bed.

"Only us," she repeated as he dropped down to kiss her.

CHAPTER 5

Sam stretched and enjoyed the slight discomfort after a night of blissful sex. She turned to see Ken on the pillow beside her. His face was completely relaxed. He was a beautiful man. The women who had made him feel less than the wonderful person he was should be drawn and quartered. Sam blinked. Well, hell, that was a bit extreme. She smiled as she stared at the man beside her. Ken had a way of making her feel protective. Anyone who would purposefully hurt him, the one with a heart that bled for little kids and victims, well, they could go to hell.

She glanced past Ken to the clock. They'd slept in. It was almost seven in the morning, way past her normal wake-up time. She slipped out of bed and grabbed his t-shirt. It fell just past her bottom and would have to do because she had no idea where ... oh, there ... She grabbed her panties and tiptoed out the door.

Slipping the t-shirt on, she breathed in the scent of the man she'd spent the night with. A smile spread across her face. If she had her way, she'd spend a whole hell of a lot more nights in his bed. The relationship was comfortable. They were friends, now lovers, and hey, they could relate to each other's job and the stress that came with it. The job was a large portion of both of their lives. For her, having someone she could vent to or laugh with was like the mortar between the bricks of their relationship. It held the brick firmly in place. It was something that had been missing in other relationships. The drafts that blew through the cracks with other boyfriends had eventually weakened the foundation. And their bricks tumbled easily with the first strong wind. Not so with Ken. With him, it was different. Stronger. Better.

After using the bathroom and combing out her hair with her fingers, she made her way into the kitchen and started a pot of coffee. Sam opened the front door, and the coolness of the morning wafted past her into the house. The fresh scent of nature filled her lungs. Closing her eyes, she absorbed the sweet sounds of early morning bird song. The peace of Ken's home filled her with a sense of contentment, refreshing her in a way she'd never felt. When the coffee pot stopped gurgling, she padded back into the kitchen and pulled a cup down. The sound of a vehicle coming down the road drew her eyes from the coffee she poured into her cup.

Sam glanced down at her attire. She didn't want to wake Ken up, but depending on who popped out of that truck ... Placing the carafe back onto the hotplate, Sam edged away from the window and got ready to sprint out of sight. Ah, no. No, she wasn't going anywhere. Allison was visible inside the truck. A hundred thoughts collided at once, and none ended well for the lady currently getting out of the vehicle.

Picking up her coffee cup, Sam walked to the front door, and when Allison looked up, she stuttered to a stop.

"Good morning, Allison. How are you this morning?" Sam heard movement in the back of the house. It didn't matter; she'd handle it. Ken didn't need the hassle of an unexpected visit.

"What are you doing here?" Allison's puzzled expression was comical.

"I'm drinking coffee at the moment. Did you bring something?" Sam looked at the white box in her hands. "I can give it to Ken for you."

Allison gave a harsh laugh. "Wow, you worked fast, didn't you?"

Sam took a drink of her coffee and narrowed her eyes. Partially because of the fact that her coffee didn't have cream and sugar, but more so at the words Allison just flung her way. "You know, I don't think I like your tone. Are you implying something?" She wasn't going to play high school games.

"He's not the man you think he is." Allison put the box down on the table by the rocker.

Sam laughed aloud at that comment. "Oh, sweetheart, he's every inch the man *I think* he is. You, however, have a very skewed and misinformed view of him." Sam sipped her coffee, gauging the woman across from her. She could sense Allison's irritation. Clearly, the morning wasn't going as the woman had planned.

"Do you know what he did?"

"What? That he kissed a girl when he was dating you?" Sam laughed again and leaned against the door frame, blocking Allison's view of the house behind her because she could hear Ken coming down the hall.

"He cheated on me."

"By kissing a girl. Woman, I don't know what fairy tale you were or are living in, but that isn't cheating. That's a young man making a mistake. But, whatever, your loss is my gain."

"He'll hurt you, too." Allison crossed her arms as her eyes misted with tears.

Sam set her cup of coffee on the table beside the box Allison had placed there. She sighed. "Oh, sweetie. Do you have any proof of that? Any at all? He was seventeen. He's a man now. A man of integrity and honor. If you still think he'd cheat, that baked good offering you brought out this morning wasn't really necessary, was it?"

Allison shoved her hands into her jeans, sniffed, and shook her head. "No. Probably not."

Sam smiled sadly. "Allison, I don't want drama. I don't have a beef with you. But honestly, you're living in the past. You need to relocate to the present and figure out what the hell you want. Ken is no longer on the market. That brilliant, funny, sexy as hell man is *mine*. We have the start of a good relationship, and you will not edge your way between us. There's no room for that to happen. He's over you, and if you look deep, you know you're over him, too. And when you've come to grips with all that, we'll welcome you back to visit and be a friend."

Allison stared at her for a long moment before running to her truck with a sob. Sam watched as Allison turned the truck around and drove away.

When she couldn't see the truck any longer, she asked, "How much did you hear?"

Ken's hand landed on her hip, and his warm body came against her back. "Most of it. I hate that it had to happen, but thank you."

She turned and slipped her arms around him. He wore jeans and was commando by the look of the unfastened and partially unzipped jeans. "She needs some help coming to grips with the fact that she can't play with your heart anymore."

"I think you set her straight." Ken lowered his head for a kiss.

When he pulled away, she smiled up at him. "Not running away because of the possessiveness I splattered all over the place?"

"I think the only person who didn't like what you were throwing around was Allison." He sighed. "I don't understand the rationale of coming out here this morning. She hasn't been here in, hell, fifteen years."

"Oh, I know why she was here."

"Do tell," Ken said as he looked down at her.

"She saw us together and happy at the diner. Then, I'm sure her mom and/or dad told her about seeing us in the store. She realized you were moving on, and that was something she didn't want. She came out here to hook you through the nose again and lead you around like some show bull."

He stared at her. "You realize she couldn't even before you came into my life. I was over her. Now that you're here, the impossibility of that scheme is astounding."

"I know." She toed up and kissed him. "But she knows now, too, which will make your life a bit messy."

Ken's brow furrowed. "How's that?"

"She's going to internalize everything I said and maybe bemoan what happened this morning to her friends. They may get snarky."

Ken rolled his eyes. "Her friends are my friends. If they get snarky, I'll call them on it. It won't be a problem."

Sam doubted that. It had been her experience

that friends stuck together, so he'd probably get some passive-aggressive comments, and so would she, but Ken was worth the attitude and the effort. She turned, breaking free of his embrace, and picked up the box Allison had left, lifting the lid carefully.

"Is it a bomb?" Ken whispered, making her laugh.

"Nope." They were muffins of some sort. She opened the flap farther so he could see. Sam sniffed the air. "Banana. Do you think they're safe to eat?"

"I think I'm willing to risk it. Let's grab a cup of coffee and gamble on them not being poisoned." Ken grabbed her cup and tossed the cold liquid into the flower bed by the door. "Flowers like coffee."

"Yeah, I'm not sure that's true." Sam followed him with the muffins.

"Has to be. I throw a little on those irises every day. They're growing like gangbusters."

"Isn't that messy in the winter?" Sam said as she retrieved two napkins.

"I don't do it in the winter." Ken laughed as he filled a cup for himself and refilled hers. "You didn't have creamer or sugar in that cup."

"I'd just poured my coffee when Allison drove up the road. I was tucked away and ready to bolt back to the bedroom, but then I saw who it was and figured I'd handle it."

"Hopefully, that ends it." Ken took a muffin and nodded to the porch. "Grab your cream and sugar. Sitting outside is the best way to drink morning coffee."

After Sam fixed her coffee to her liking, they went to the porch. Ken gave her the rocker and sat on the bench next to it. "I was enjoying the bird song earlier. My apartment doesn't have the orchestra you have out here."

"This centers me. No matter what the day before has landed on my lap, waking up here and listening to nature, or in the winter watching the snow fall sitting by the fireplace and drinking my coffee, well, it reminds me that we're just a small part of this world." Ken took a bite of the muffin. He chewed it, and after he swallowed, he shrugged. "I don't taste any poison."

Sam lifted her eyebrows. "Cool. I'll give it a minute to make sure."

Ken barked out a laugh. "What do you feel like doing today?"

"Show me your turkey hunting grounds. I want to know the type of gear to wear."

"Definitely hiking boots. We'll go south and east. The Marshalls' land is where I usually hunt. Frank doesn't mind as long as I let him know where I'll be, so his hands don't wander out into a tree claim I'm working."

"I like him. Mr. Marshall." Sam pushed her bare toe against the wood decking and took a bite of her muffin as she rocked backward.

"Yeah. The Marshalls are good people."

"You should talk to him about running for sheriff."

"It's tempting and an honor, but I think it may be too much of a gamble." Ken shook his head. "I don't know how to be anything but what I am."

Sam wouldn't push him. It was his decision. "All right, but it can't hurt to talk. Hear him out and then politely say thanks, but no thanks. It's the right thing to do."

Ken nodded and took a sip of his coffee. "Figured I'd wander out to the ranch Monday or Tuesday and have a word or two."

She nodded and took a sip of her coffee. "If we head south to check out the hunting grounds, we can take two vehicles, and I'll head back. I need to do laundry and iron this week's uniforms before tomorrow morning."

Ken glanced over at her. "You should bring some uniforms up here. In case you work late or, you know, want to stay over."

She picked off a bit of muffin with her fingers. "You wouldn't mind?"

"Nope." He popped the rest of his muffin in his mouth.

Sam ate the bite she had in her fingers and smiled. She liked that invitation. She liked it a lot.

"When do you want to head south?" Ken asked.

"After lunch?" She shrugged.

"Good. Then, we have time."

"Time for what?" she said with a smile.

"I wanted to introduce you to my shower." Standing, Ken extended his hand to her.

"Oh? Do we need an introduction?"

"Definitely. You might be spending an extended period in it this morning."

"Are you inviting me into your shower?"

"Nope." Ken swooped down and picked her up, tossing her over his shoulder.

"Ken!" she shrieked and then laughed as she dangled down his back. "Let me down! I'm too heavy!"

"You're not. Get that door, will you?" He paused just inside the front door. Sam laughed and pushed the door shut behind them.

"You're insane." She braced her hands on his ass and lifted a bit.

"Crazy for you," Ken crowed.

"Dork." Sam snorted because she was laughing so hard. She slapped her hand over her mouth and disintegrated into a fit of giggles. Being with Ken was easy and fun. She'd found a keeper.

CHAPTER 6

Ken didn't have to go to the Marshall Ranch. Monday morning, he was sitting at the diner enjoying his usual with Alex when Frank Marshall and the senior Hollister pulled up simultaneously. Something was up. On two fingers, he could count the times Senior and Frank had been to town that early in the past fifteen years. One was the tornado that almost took out the town, and the other was today.

Alex looked up from his breakfast. "What?"

Ken blinked. "Huh?" he asked.

"You said, 'damn it'." Alex picked up his milk.

"Ah, nothing. Just going to have a conversation a bit before I'm prepared for it."

Alex's eyes popped open. "Dude, I feel that on a cellular level. Don't mess with my schedule."

"Right?" Ken chuckled.

"More coffee?" Ciera came out of the kitchen with a pot.

"Thank you, but I just refilled." Ken lifted his full cup.

Ciera turned when the bell over the door jingled. "Hi, Mr. Marshall. Mr. Hollister. Can I get you breakfast?"

"Two of those truck-sized cinnamon rolls and a pot of coffee, please," Senior said as the men walked in. "Ken, can we have a moment?" he asked as they shut the door behind them.

"That's my cue to leave." Alex wiped his mouth, dropped his money on the counter, and nodded at the men. "Gentlemen, have a good day."

"Alex." As Frank Marshall nodded, Senior smiled, and they took a seat on either side of Ken. Senior pushed Alex's dishes down the counter. "So, Frank told me he let the cat out of the bag."

Ken glanced to his left. "Yes, sir. He mentioned he'd like me to consider running for sheriff." Thank God there wasn't anyone else in the diner at the moment. If there were, that tidbit of information would be spread far and wide faster than a person could whistle.

Ciera appeared with two massive cinnamon rolls and poured two cups of coffee. "Cream or sugar?"

"'Nuff sugar in the rolls for me. Thank you," Frank said and took a sip of his coffee.

"I'll take both," Senior said. She put down a small silver pitcher and a holder with small sugar packets in front of him. The men waited until Ciera collected Alex's plates and returned to the kitchen.

"What do you think about the idea?"

"I'm concerned about several points." Ken stared straight ahead. "If I run and lose, Colby would make my life hell. I'd have to find another job." That was the long pole in the tent, for sure. He'd rolled that thought around, and all kinds of insecurity stuck to it. He didn't want to leave Hollister. It was his home. Add to that his new and damn good relationship with Sam, and there was no way in hell he'd leave to take another job.

"He won't win." Senior cut off a hunk of his roll. "The only reason he's in office now is because no one would oppose him. You're our man, Ken.

You're better than that blowhard. You know everyone in the county."

"Not true. There are people up north I haven't met."

"Very few," Senior said before taking his bite of roll. "Damn, these things are good." The man shook his head.

"I don't have the money to run a campaign. Posters and billboards and such." Ken shook his head. "Colby reuses the ones he has printed. I see him picking them up every year."

"In his patrol vehicle." Frank chuckled.

"He's authorized." Ken didn't want them to think he wasn't. "The county lets him, and the senior deputies can use their vehicles for personal use."

"Know it." Frank nodded. "Don't care if you use your vehicle. For you, I'd pay for gas all day, every day. You work your ass off. The problem I have is Colby does nothing but sit in that office. He talks on the phone and surfs the internet all day." Frank looked around the diner. "I heard he's looking at sites I don't want any of my elected officials looking at—ever. He doesn't clear his search history either."

Ken closed his eyes. He didn't need to hear that. "Illegal?"

Frank grunted. Senior said, "That was a yes."

"I'll need to cite how I got the information to get a search warrant." He wouldn't do an illegal search on the boss's computer. That would get the case thrown out and him fired.

Frank took a long breath and turned to him. "If you were to know when he was on the computer and happened to walk in on him and see what he was looking at, would you need to cite your source?"

Ken thought about that for a minute. He could use his discovery as a means to get a court order.

"You're sure this will work?" Ken sighed.

"Yep," Senior and Frank said at the same time.

"The county commissioners support you as interim sheriff. The decision is made by the governor, though. Colby answers for the things he's doing, then you run for the office of sheriff. Unopposed," Senior added.

Ken picked up his coffee. Lord, there was no way he couldn't act. If what Mr. Marshall had alluded to was true, Colby needed to face the music. He'd have to be careful about how he went about it, but he'd get the job done. Shit. He was going to do it, wasn't he? Yes. Hell, yes. It wasn't about him running for sheriff. It was about doing what he swore to do when he put on the badge. He was going to hold a criminal accountable for his actions. He shook his head and sighed. "You've backed me into a corner."

"Hell of a thing. Using their good morals and sincere integrity against a person. Shame on you, Frank." Senior chuckled.

Frank grunted. "Ken is the man who should lead in that office. When I discovered what was happening, I knew who needed to take over this county."

The bell above the door jingled again, and all three men turned toward the door. Tegan Wells and a couple of the hands from the stockyard walked in. They said their hellos and sat down at a booth.

Ken lowered his voice. "I'll do it."

"Knew you would. You just needed all the information. If you'd hesitated, I would have had it reported to the proper authorities, but I'll trust you to take care of matters." Frank drank the last of his coffee. "If you need backup, you know where to look."

"Yes, sir. I do, and I'll take you up on that offer."

He wasn't a fool. Or maybe he was. Shit, at that point, he wasn't sure.

Things moved fast after that. About two hours later, he received a text that Colby was on the computer. Ken was halfway to the sheriff's station when he got the text. He had no idea who it came from. It wasn't a local number. He pulled over and texted back:

> Twenty minutes out. Let me know if he logs out.

> Affirmative.

KEN SIGHED and put the SUV into gear. He hated like hell that the sheriff had put him in that position. Twenty minutes later, he pulled into the parking lot of the sheriff's office and sent a text.

> Still online?

KEN

. . .

> Affirmative.

Ken pocketed his phone and strolled into the building.

"Hey, Ken." Dot McShane smiled at him. She was the sheriff's gatekeeper and the daytime dispatcher. They used a regional dispatcher for after-hour calls. The counties had pitched in together to purchase the service. Since Dot was getting a paycheck for the nine-to-five gig, she handled anything that happened during the day.

"Hi, Dot. How are you doing today?"

"I'm good. You here to see Colby?"

Ken shook his head. "Nah, just stopping by to visit my favorite girl."

Dot blushed and swatted at him. "I'm almost sixty-seven years old. Go find yourself a sweet young thing." Ken grinned. He couldn't help himself. Sam's smile filled his thoughts for a nano second before the image of her naked body flashed through his mind. He could feel his face turn hot and knew he was red. Dot blinked up at him. "Oh, goodness, you did, didn't you?" Dot put her hand over her ample chest. "That just makes my heart sing. Tell me all about it!"

"Do you have fresh coffee?" Ken had seen the pot was almost empty when he walked in.

"No, but I can make a pot. You just sit right here; I'll be right back." The woman twittered like a bird as she headed to the break room.

Ken waited until Dot had gone into the room, then moved. He walked down the hall, opened the door to the sheriff's office, and ...

"Holy fuck!" Colby shouted.

Ken froze and stared at the scene. Colby's pants were down around his knees. His hand was on his erect cock, and the image on the screen made Ken want to vomit.

Dot rushed in behind him. "What's wrong? Oh, oh my God, no." The woman gasped and then saw the computer screen. "You're sick!" she screamed at Colby.

"Dot, go to your desk. I'll handle this," Ken ordered as Colby shoved himself back into his pants.

"I can explain. This isn't what it looks like."

"Colby Reicher, you are under arrest for possession of child pornography." Ken walked up and spun the older man, slapping handcuffs on the sheriff before the man could move. "Dot, call the state police and ask for an investigator to be dispatched immediately."

"You can't do this. I haven't done anything wrong!" Colby shouted.

Ken spun him toward the computer screen. "That girl didn't do anything wrong either, and sick bastards like you still exploit them. You have the right to remain silent, and I strongly suggest you use it, Colby. Your computer will testify against you." He finished giving the sheriff his Miranda Rights, allowed him to pull up his pants, and then re-cuffed him.

Dot came back down the hall. "Is it safe to come in?"

"Yeah, just don't look at the computer," Ken said.

"The state police have someone in Rapid who's finishing up a case. They'll be here in three hours. I gave them your cell phone number to call for any questions." Dot had tears rolling down her face as she turned to the sheriff. "Why would you do such a thing, Colby? What about your wife and your daughters? You have granddaughters, for God's sake."

The sheriff looked down, unable to meet Dot's gaze.

"Dot, could you do me a favor and keep this quiet?" Ken said. "We aren't making this public. Mable and the girls don't need that to happen before they find out what's going on."

Dot sniffed. "I understand." She straightened her shoulders. "I won't say a word unless you tell me to."

"I want you to write down everything that happened and exactly what you saw." Ken felt the man he was holding by the arm deflate as the realization of what happened sank in.

"I will." She looked at Colby. "Everything." She left the doorway and walked down the hall.

Colby's voice shook as he spoke. "You don't have to do this, Ken. I can smooth things over with Dot. Hell, I'll give you a pay raise. I've been sitting on a bit of money for emergencies."

"Don't add bribery to the list of charges, Colby. Please, for your sake, shut the fuck up and wait until you can call a lawyer. You're going to need it."

His cell phone vibrated. He didn't recognize the number. "Deputy Zorn."

"Deputy, this is Warren Carson. I'm the deputy commander of the South Dakota Bureau of Investigations. Can you give me a rundown of what we're looking at?"

"Just a minute, sir." He moved Colby away from the computer and kicked the desk chair over to the corner of the room. "Sit down and don't move, or I'll put you in the holding cell." It was basically a closet where they'd fashioned a bench and reinforced the door, but they could hold someone there if needed.

"I came to the station to have coffee with Dot, the secretary. I had some good news to share, and I thought I'd tell the sheriff at the same time." Ken looked over at Colby. He'd found a place on the floor to stare at. "I opened the door to the sheriff's office and found him in a state of undress and sexually aroused while viewing a picture of a girl way under the age of eighteen."

"The picture is on his computer?" Warren Carson asked.

"Yes, sir. His county-issued computer." The stupid, sick fool.

"His *work* computer?" Warren asked again.

"Yes, sir," Ken confirmed, looking at the paper inventory label on the screen.

"There is no expectation of privacy on a work computer. That's the read the federal courts have upheld. We'll still get a warrant, but he didn't make this difficult. Who's the senior deputy in the county?"

"I am, sir. Also, the secretary witnessed everything, including the picture on the computer." Ken drove that nail into Colby's coffin. The man would never hold public office again. If he lived through the jail time he'd receive. Most prisons weren't hospitable to child pornographers.

"All right. Investigator Makala Dennis is on her way up from Rapid City. She'll take custody of the computer, and we'll bring it back for a complete forensics review. You'll need to book the sheriff. Will that be a problem?"

"No, sir. I'll head down to Belle with him when your investigator arrives. I'll also complete my statement and ensure the secretary's is done, too. We have an agreement with Butte County to hold our detainees until they're arraigned."

"I'll call Butte County's sheriff and tell him you'll be down and what you're handling."

"Thank you. Sir, what about his family?"

There was a long sigh at the other end of the connection. "It sucks for them, for sure. We'll get a search warrant for his home, cell phone, and any vehicles he may have. Does he drive a county vehicle?"

"Yes, sir."

"Impound it. I don't want the family notified until we issue the search warrant on his house. On second thought, do you have a holding cell?"

"Yes, sir."

"Here's the plan. I'm asking you to help our investigator with the search of the sheriff's house. Place him in your holding cell. You can take him to Belle Fourche when you finish the search warrant. It'll be a long day for you, deputy, but I don't want anything slipping out of our fingers."

"I understand." He couldn't imagine Mable hiding anything from them, but then again, people were peculiar at times.

* * *

THE SUN HAD SET, and the stars were starting to pop against the darkening sky. Ken glanced down at his watch. Shit, it had been ten hours since he'd walked into the station, and now, he was walking out of the Butte County Jail.

Colby had cussed, cried, begged, and pleaded with

him the entire way to Belle Fourche. Ken didn't speak a word to the man except for the few things he needed to say to book Colby into jail. He knew what he and the investigator had found at the house. He had to call Zeke Johnson over to Colby and Mable's house. Mable was having chest pains. The woman was beyond distraught because, when they opened the closet that Colby kept his hunting things in, they'd found a box of pictures. Mable saw them, and yeah, they were more of the same. His home computer was unplugged, tagged, and placed in the trunk of the investigator's vehicle. Colby's personal cell phone and tablet were taken as well. Mable gave them the code to open the devices. He didn't look. He didn't want to know. The evidence they had was more than enough to put Colby behind bars for years.

"Tell him not to come back here," Mable said weakly from the couch.

"Yes, ma'am," Ken said and knelt in front of her. "Are either of your daughters coming up to be with you?"

"Melissa is tomorrow. I'll lock up and go with her back to Custer. Here." She handed him a key. "You have my permission to come back and search through anything at any time."

He looked up at the investigator, who nodded before saying, "We'll need that in writing."

Ken helped Mable with the consent, and by the time they were done, the investigator was finished with her notes.

"Doc Johnson said you'd be okay, but how about I call Dot over to stay with you?" Ken asked.

"Does she know?" Mable's eyes held a pain that he understood but couldn't fathom.

He nodded. "She does, but we're the only two. The governor will have to convene a special hearing, and then, if he relieves Colby, he'll notify the county commissioners. Then someone will be appointed to replace Colby until he's convicted."

"Is there a chance they won't relieve or convict him?"

Ken shook his head. "Think about what you saw, Mable. We followed the law to obtain the evidence."

She nodded and wiped at a tear. "He needs to pay for what he's done. He isn't the man I married. I just can't fathom why ..." She grabbed a tissue and wiped her nose. "Anyway, I'll be gone by the time everyone knows." Mable nodded to herself. "You let them know I had no idea. Will you?"

"I promise. This is your home, Mable. You don't need to leave." Ken put his hand on hers.

"It isn't the home I thought it was." A tear fell down her cheek. "How could he do that? Why?"

"I don't know. I don't. I'll call Dot."

"Thank you, Ken." Mable sniffed and wiped at the tear. "He's going to stay in jail?"

"Unless the judge lets him out on bail."

"He'd have to have someone post that for him, right?"

"Yes, ma'am."

"Then he'll stay in jail. I won't be using any money to post bail." She shivered. "I saw what was in that box. I have daughters. *We* have daughters and granddaughters. My God." She buried her face in her hands and cried. Ken let her have a moment as he placed the call to Dot.

"Hello?"

"Dot, could you come over to Mable's? She needs someone to stay with her until her daughter comes tomorrow to take her south."

"Of course. How's she taking it?"

"Not well. It was a shock."

Dot sighed, "Yeah, that's the truth of the matter, isn't it? Tell her I'll be over. We can stare at the wall together. Why would he do such a thing?"

"I wish I knew, Dot. I wish I knew." Ken disconnected the call and helped the investigator by transporting items from the home to the vehicle, who inventoried everything one last time before shutting the trunk.

"Deputy, I'm sorry you had to deal with this."

"I'm sorry anyone had to." Ken shook her hand. "You have my number if you need anything."

"I do. I'm going to head down to Belle and grab a hotel for the night. I'll follow you down."

"Sounds like a plan."

The weight of what Colby had done hung around the necks of his wife and his family, and as soon as the charges were released, they would settle around all those who knew him. Ken's chest hurt. He was grieving. He was grieving for the people of the county, the children affected by the horrible photos, and the loss of a man he thought he knew. Colby gave Ken a chance when he was a young man. That man he would grieve. Not the man he saw that day. The crimes Colby committed could never be forgotten or forgiven. Colby was a predator of the worst sort. He victimized the young and innocent and had needlessly torn apart countless lives.

* * *

Ken zombie shuffled to his patrol car. The booking process was behind him, but the weight of what had transpired hadn't lessened.

"Hey, stranger." Ken jolted and turned at the greeting. "It's just me," Sam said from where she stood. Her old SUV was parked next to his. "I heard through the grapevine that you had a bad day."

Ken walked up to her and pulled her into his arms. Fuck, he needed to feel that. He held her tightly. "I don't know how to explain how bad it was."

"Why don't you come over to my apartment tonight? You don't need to drive back. Someone's covering for you, right?"

"Yeah. Garth. We pulled him as a temporary full-time until we can get things sorted."

"Then follow me. I'll feed you, pour you a strong drink, listen to what happened, and give you something good to think about." She toed up and kissed him.

Ken took control of the kiss and grabbed her hair in his fists. It splayed across his arms in a tumble of waves. He lifted away and stared down at her. "I don't deserve you."

"That's where you're so very wrong. Let's get you out of the monkey suit and get some food into you. Have you eaten at all today?" she said as she walked him to his SUV.

"Breakfast, but that seems like a lifetime ago." His head was pounding.

"No doubt. Follow me, deputy." She walked over to her vehicle and got in. Ken didn't even consider doing anything but what she'd told him to do. Frankly, he didn't have the capacity to drive back to Hollister at that point. He followed her to the apartment complex, where he pulled into a slot beside her patrol vehicle.

After getting out of her SUV, he walked into Sam's first-floor apartment. Smiling, he noted it was just as sparsely decorated as his place. She tossed her keys into a bowl by the door and pulled her service weapon from the back holster she had clipped to her belt. "Why don't you shower while I get dinner going?"

Ken looked down at his uniform. "I have a gym bag in the back of the SUV with a change of clothes."

She stopped and looked at him. "Why?"

He chuckled and rubbed the back of his neck. "I've been covered in mud, sprayed by a skunk, caught in a downpour, ran through pastures filled with manure, and almost every other conceivable circumstance in the last fifteen years. I learned my lesson."

"Well, give me your keys, take off the gun belt, and shower. I'll bring your bag in."

He handed her his keys but caught her hand as she reached for them. He pulled her in for a kiss, and she melted into him. Her body was made for his. He broke the kiss. "You should wait for dinner and join me in the shower."

"That sounds like a fun time, but there's a problem with that. Besides, tonight, I'm going to take care of you." She leaned up and pecked him on the lips. "I promise it'll be worth it."

Ken let her go and made a face when the door shut. "I don't know. Shower sex sounds amazing." After taking off his gun belt and boots, he found the bathroom. Well, *that* could be the reason she said no. The shower was almost big enough to hold him. Almost. He'd been on airplanes with bigger bathrooms. Okay, not really, but damn, it was tight. He took off his uniform and folded it carefully before stepping into the shower. The hot water and damn good water pressure made the cramped quarters a little more bearable.

He used her shampoo. Thankfully, it didn't smell like flowers. The door opened, and he felt the drift of cooler air. He opened one eye.

"I'm going to have to find a place with a bigger shower." She sighed and set his bag down. "I'll hang up your uniform."

"Thank you. I'll be out in a minute." He shoved his head under the water and rinsed out the shampoo.

It took him a couple of minutes to finish and get out of the shower. He pulled on an old pair of jeans and a t-shirt he used as backup clothes. Barefoot, he made his way back to the small front room and kitchen. "Smells good," he said as she offered him a glass. Thinking it was soda, he took a big gulp. The alcohol burned on the way down. "Wow." He coughed and put the glass down.

She smiled at him. "Gentleman Jack and Coke. More Gentleman than Coke."

"Yeah, I got that." Ken cleared his throat. "Thanks."

Sam laughed and flipped her hair over her shoulder. "No problem. Have a seat. I'll have this out of the oven in a second."

Ken pulled out a chair and sat down. Then he took another sip of his drink. "So, tell me about it." Samantha moved around the efficiency kitchen as she made a salad.

"Got a tip that the sheriff may have been using his computer in a way he shouldn't. So, I went to the station. Got the secretary, who's normally his door guard, to make a pot of coffee. I walked down the hall and opened the door." Ken leaned forward and stared at his drink. "He was jacking off to a picture of a little girl. It was on his computer. The secretary saw it, too. I arrested him, and we called in the state investigators. Searched his house, took all his electronics, and, when we went into a closet that he said held his hunting supplies, we found a lot of guns, but it also held a box filled with photographs." Ken closed his eyes. "His wife had no idea, and unfortunately, she saw what was in the box. I had to call in Zeke Johnson because she was having chest pains. Turns out it was an anxiety attack, but …" He hated what Colby's shit had done to his wife.

Sam's hands landed softly on his shoulders, and she kissed the top of his head. "I know it sucked for you today. I'm so sorry you had to deal with it alone."

"This helps." He put his hand over hers. "Having someone who you trust to unload all of this ... someone who understands, it really helps." He squeezed her hand when the timer on the microwave went off. Though she moved across the kitchen, the space didn't sever the connection between them. A platter of chicken and potatoes landed in front of him a few moments later.

"Was Colby compliant?"

"Yes and no. At first, he tried to tell me it wasn't what I thought it was." Ken picked up his fork and stabbed at the fluffy potatoes, shaking his head. "It was exactly what I thought it was."

"Who tipped you off?"

Ken lifted his eyes. "Doesn't matter. I walked in and saw the evidence with my own eyes. My tip was moot as soon as that happened."

Sam put a salad she'd dressed in front of him. "True, but that isn't what I asked."

"Would you be upset if I told you that, respectfully, I'm going to decline to answer that?"

Sam cocked her head at him. "No. Not at all. I was just wondering how they knew."

Ken snorted and picked up a chicken leg. "Me, too." He took a bite, and his stomach finally figured out it had been over twelve hours since he'd eaten. "This is good."

"Thank you."

They ate, and Sam asked questions about the search. He detailed how the state investigator searched each room, following the search warrant to the letter. "She's sharp. You could tell this wasn't her first rodeo."

"Should I be jealous?" Sam asked as she got a bottle of wine out and poured herself a glass.

"No." Ken felt himself blush. "There isn't any reason for you to be jealous."

Sam walked over and kissed him. "Right answer, Deputy Zorn."

He finished his meal and the extra strong drink. "You know, I think the thing that bothers me the most is I trusted this guy."

"You feel violated. It's understandable. Hell, he was a cop. I feel like he smeared all of us with his tainted brush." Sam stood and took his glass, pouring him another drink.

"Not as strong, please."

She smiled and winked at him. "Trust me."

He took the drink and then followed her into the living room. "Everyone kept asking me why. I wish I had an answer for them. How can a person explain acts like that when understanding it is something I can't even conceptually grasp."

Sam sat down beside him. "Explaining it is his worry, not yours. He lost everything today. His job, his wife, and probably his freedom. He's the one who needs to explain, not you."

Ken nodded and took another gulp from his drink before dropping his arm over her shoulders. "Today sucked."

She nodded. "I missed seeing you on the road today. Knew it had to be something big. I stopped at Hollister, and Tegan was at the hardware store. He said he saw you at breakfast. There hadn't been any requests for assistance, so I buried my head in the sand and figured I'd call tonight. When I got back down here, the rumor mill was churning. You know cops; we're worse than Edna and Phil combined."

Ken chuckled. "That we are."

She leaned her head back on his shoulder and looked up at him. "Feeling a bit better?"

"The headache has subsided." He nodded. "I'm full and a bit tipsy."

"Good. Just what I wanted." She stood up and extended her hand to him. "On to the next phase of my dastardly plan."

"Should I be worried?" Ken asked as he took her hand and stood up.

"Not even a little bit." Sam led him back to the bedroom. "Take off your clothes, face first, onto the bed."

Ken lifted an eyebrow at her. "Okay, now, I'm a little bit worried."

Sam belted out a laugh. "I'm going to give you a massage, sir. What do you think I am, a dominatrix or something?"

Ken pulled off his shirt. "Since I'm not quite sure I have adequate knowledge of what a dominatrix is or does, I'm invoking my rights against self-incrimination." He watched as she went into the tiny bathroom and heard her laughter as the cabinets banged shut.

He laid down on the top of the soft duvet and pulled a pillow under his chest. He turned his head when he heard Sam come back into the room. She'd pulled her hair up in a ponytail and was taking off her jeans. "A dominatrix is a woman who uses control and sometimes pain to inflict pleasure on her submissive."

Ken narrowed his eyes at her. "Yeah, that's what I thought it was. Not at all interested in that."

"Thank God!" Sam laughed and poured oil into

her hand. "Now, relax, and just let me make you feel better." She grabbed his foot and started to knead it. The groan that pushed out of his lungs was nothing but pure pleasure.

"Oh, for the love of everything, don't stop."

Sam chuckled and continued her ministrations. Ken thought he knew pleasure, but that definition changed when she moved from his feet to his calves. He melted under her touch as she moved up, oiling her hands as she advanced to his thighs. He chuckled a bit as she massaged his ass, but if he was honest, it felt amazing. By the time she got to the small of his back, he was hers to do with as she pleased. She'd stopped talking halfway up his legs, and he started to drift. There were no problems. Nothing but sensation filled his mind. He jumped a couple of times, jerking himself from sleep. Sam kept working the muscles in his back. He didn't deserve the special attention … but it was … nice …

CHAPTER 7

Ken moved away from whatever was tickling his nose and settled back to sleep. Only the tickle didn't leave. He cracked his eye open and then blinked rapidly, jerking back a bit. Sam's hair covered his face. Lifting a bit, he found himself on his stomach. Sam was in the bed with him under the sheet. He blinked and looked at the clock. Five in the morning. He dropped his head back down on the pillow covered in auburn hair.

Sam woke with a start. "It's okay," he said in a voice that sounded more toad than human.

She tried to turn, but her hair was under him. He lifted, and she was able to roll. "Good morning." She snuggled closer, but the sheet kept her beautiful body from pressing against his. He could remedy that.

"Not yet." He hiked up and jerked the sheet out from under himself before he flopped it over him. He belted his arms around her and pulled her into him. Her warm, soft skin melded to him, and he sighed. "Now, it's a good morning. You should have woken me up."

"Nope. I was hoping you'd shut down. You had a lot to deal with yesterday, and I'm wagering today won't be much better."

Ken closed his eyes and drew a deep breath. It wouldn't be better. All the questions would start, and he'd have to put a stop to it immediately. He wouldn't let the investigation become local gossip fodder. Well, any more than it was. No one from his department would talk. He'd already spoken to Dot about keeping everything quiet. She was more than happy to comply. The fact that Colby had been jerking off in his office while she guarded the door had been a personal violation for her. Dot was a vault when she needed to be. Ken sighed again. "Thank you. I fell asleep before I could say that. I've never had anyone …" Hell, how did he explain it without sounding pathetic? He couldn't. "Never mind."

Sam arched to look up at him. "Never had anyone treat you like you mattered?"

Ken stared down at her. "I have friends who watch out for me, but what happened last night was … amazing."

Sam smiled up at him. "If I had a miserable day, you'd do the same for me, right?"

"I would've tried to make it better, yes. I'm not sure my massage skills are as good as yours." As he dropped down for a kiss, her arms wrapped around his neck, and his morning wood kicked to life.

"Do we have time?" Sam purred when he pulled away from their kiss.

"What time do you have to be on the road?"

"Seven."

"Then, we have time." Ken dropped back down. Her hands went down his back when he moved to her ear. He pushed up and slid over the top of her, and she opened her legs to let him settle between them. She cradled him, and his eyes could have rolled backward into his brain at the perfection of the feeling.

"Can I make a suggestion?"

Ken stopped and lifted to his elbows. "Anything."

"Let me up." She pushed him gently and moved. Sam rolled and lifted onto her hands and knees. She looked over her shoulder at him and whispered, "Come here."

Ken did not have to be told twice. He was behind her marvelous ass in a heartbeat. He ran his hand up her spine and grabbed a handful of that luxurious mane as he lined up his cock to her core. She moved backward when she felt the tip, and he grabbed her hips. Fuck, the feel of her heat was incendiary. When he thrust forward, she pushed back. His grip tightened on her hip and in her hair. She lowered her shoulders to the bed, and he was fucking lost. The visual of her body completely at his will was heady and powerful. As he got closer, he bent over her, pulled her onto her knees, and then up and back into his chest. He cupped her breast in one hand and trailed the other hand lower. He found her clit and rubbed the nub between his fingers. She jerked, and he clasped her tighter to his body.

The ability to hold that strong woman was life changing. He was the one making her writhe against his body. He was the one making her gasp and moan those sounds of pleasure and want. He'd never felt so powerful. He felt her tighten around him, yet he didn't slow down. The potent energy that flowed through him was a new awakening. She had returned a part of himself he'd lost somewhere. He found himself with her. His hips raced with urgency, and he exploded, the white-hot pool at the base of his spine shattered, and he crashed into the bliss of orgasm. He caught himself on one arm, holding Samantha with the other as they panted and raked in air. God, he was falling in love with her. Hell, who was he fooling? He'd been halfway in love with her for months.

He controlled their descent into the bed and pulled her into him. "That was …" He panted for air.

"Fucking amazing," she supplied.

"Yeah, that," he agreed and wiped at the sweat on his forehead. "Cardio is done for the day."

She laughed and nodded. "Definitely." She turned so she could see him. "You were a beast."

He lost the smile. "Did I—"

"No," she interrupted. "A sexy beast in the best possible way. God, I'm going to feel you all day, and I'm so good with that."

Ken released the air in his chest. "I thought for a minute I'd gotten too carried away."

"No, not at all. Reference the fucking amazing

comment earlier." Sam sighed. "Can we take a nap before we go to work?"

Ken lifted to look at the clock beside her bed. "I don't think so. I'll shower first and then get breakfast going while you get ready."

"Oh, I like that arrangement. Coffee, too?"

"Nope, you get the coffee while I'm in the shower. I get the food." He kissed her on the nose.

"Well, I guess I can deal with that." She flopped over and started mock snoring. Ken swatted her on her bare ass and hopped out of bed. "Hey! So not cool!"

He laughed and headed into the tiny bathroom. He showered quickly and got out to find his boxers, travel kit, and uniform hanging up behind the door. It took him no more than ten minutes to shower and get ready. Opening the door, he saw Samantha holding a huge mug of coffee. "Thank you." He dropped a kiss on her upturned lips.

"You're welcome," she murmured as she slipped by him into the bathroom. "I'm hungry. Somehow, I worked up an appetite."

"I have no idea how that could have happened," Ken said before looking down into his mug. "Hey, half of this is gone, and it has cream and sugar."

Sam turned around and took the cup. "Oh,

dear, my mistake. You should get your own." She smirked at him as she shut the bathroom door.

Ken snickered as he headed down the hall to the kitchen. Life with that woman would never be boring. He found the frying pan and had eggs and toast done by the time she came out of the bathroom. He'd also drank a cup of coffee and was starting on mug number two. He refilled her cup and set the cream and sugar before her. "This looks amazing."

"Eggs and toast? Not too hard to make." He sat down across from her.

"Breakfast is usually a weekend thing for me. On my way north, I grab a protein drink or something quick from the truck stop."

Ken stared at her for a minute. "Are you serious? Why?"

She shrugged. "I don't know. Not having to clean dishes, or maybe eating alone sucks?"

Ken nodded as he worked his eggs onto his fork. "That's why I usually eat at the diner. At least one meal a day, but I always have toast and coffee before I start work. I'm crap without something to eat."

"When do you work out?" Sam took a bite of the eggs and made a happy hum.

"Usually at night. I'll get home and chop wood, or if it's been a bad day, I'll go for a run." Ken took a bite of his toast and glanced over at her. Her mouth was open, and her fork had stopped halfway to her mouth. "What?"

She blinked and then shook her head. "I was just picturing you without your shirt, chopping wood." She shivered. "I have to see that."

Ken felt his face go hot. She smiled at him and winked. "One of these days, you'll get used to me and stop blushing."

"Probably not." He wasn't used to anyone talking about him like that. He took a sip of his coffee. "You should probably bring up some clothes so you can spend the night up north."

Samantha glanced over at him. "I will if you bring some clothes down here for the same reason."

"I will, but in full disclosure, I'm not sure how much time I'll have to come down. The mess that's going on right now could be hectic."

"That's more than understandable, but having something here could let you be a bit spontaneous."

Ken laughed. "Yeah, that's me—Mister Spontaneous. You had to hit me over the head before I asked you to the house."

Sam smiled wide. "We'll work on that."

"I'm game." He glanced at his cell phone. "But I need to head north." He stood up and helped put the dishes in the dishwasher. His gun belt was beside hers, and they put them on simultaneously. A unique feeling of rightness made him stop and look at her. She glanced at him at the same time. "Weird, isn't it? I mean how cool is this? I've never gotten ready for work with someone who did the same thing as I do."

Sam nodded. "I was just thinking something like that." She put her last stay through her belt and snapped it into place on her leather gear. "Be safe out there, Deputy Zorn."

"Right back at you, Trooper Quinn." He leaned down to kiss her before grabbing his cowboy hat. She picked up her trooper hat and settled it on her head.

"Someday, I'm going to see how you make all that hair go into that." He pointed at her bun at the back of her head.

"How about I let you take it out some night?" She winked at him from under the brim of her hat, then put on her reflective sunglasses.

"Oh, damn. Reverse engineering. I'm game." He was game for removing her uniform, too, but he didn't say it. They walked out to their vehicles together. "I'll see you later," he said as she got into her car.

Sam's passenger side window rolled down. "You can bank on that, Deputy Zorn." She started her car and backed out of the parking spot, while he got into his SUV and followed suit with a smile plastered on his face. It had been a hell of a day yesterday, but today, well, today, started better than he could have imagined.

CHAPTER 8

Ken's phone started ringing as soon as he was on the road. He put the phone in hands-free mode and answered it. "Zorn."

"Good morning, sheriff." Senior's voice came across the speaker of his SUV.

"I'm not the sheriff," Ken reminded him.

"As of eight-thirty last night, you are. As the chair for the county commission, I got a phone call from the governor. He was briefed about Colby by the South Dakota Bureau of Investigations. Due to the amount of evidence and two witnesses to the event, he convened an emergency meeting with the state attorney, and they put Colby on administrative leave without pay. They asked for my recommendation for you to be interim sheriff. I told them there wasn't a better man in the county to fill the position. It's a temporary appointment while Colby goes through his legal issues. Congratulations."

"Will you forgive me if I'm not happy about how this came about?" Ken shook his head. "I hate it for the county and Colby's family."

"And that's why you're the best candidate for interim sheriff," Senior responded. "Now, there were a few things brought up during that meeting that I need to let you know about."

"Yes, sir." Ken was sure there were a lot of questions, but he couldn't answer them.

"While working as sheriff, you'll receive Colby's pay. That starts today. Additionally, while I was briefing each of the commissioners on what was going on, Charlie Kinzer asked for an audit of the department's books. We'll get the county auditor to come by and go through everything, from top to bottom."

"That would be good. Colby mentioned something about some funds he was sitting on yesterday." Ken wouldn't say anything else unless he was directed to do so.

"Why does that not surprise me? The audit is

overdue, but Karen O'Dell is part-time and only does what she's told. The commissioners have been remiss in our duties. We're fixing that. We want you to inherit a solid organization."

"I'm grateful," Ken said as he continued the drive north.

"Can you meet her at the station?"

"Karen? No, not right now. I'm on my way north from Belle. I spent the night there. I was too tired, mentally and physically, to drive back."

"I can understand that. I know this was hard on you, but it's better for our community in the long run."

Ken sighed. "I know. Have Karen go to the station. Dot knows where everything is. She can have full access to whatever she needs if it isn't on Colby's computer. If it is, you'll need to call SDBOI to get them to release the files. They have his computer. I'll call Dot and get the ball rolling."

"I will, and as long as she has complete access, you don't need to be present. The governor's office notified the people in the state that needed to be notified. And I'd like your opinion on something. I figured you'd want to move the station closer to Hollister. The clothing store and Allison's bakery are almost done, but I can get an office for you and the deputies made by winter."

"I appreciate that, sir, but shouldn't you wait to see who the people elect?"

"Son, I don't doubt you'll be elected, and in the wild shot you're not, you can still use the building as a substation. Our town needs law enforcement presence, but we're not big enough for a constable or a police officer. We don't have the tax base."

"You've done a lot of thinking about this, haven't you?" Ken chuckled.

"When you get to my age, you think about how you'll leave this world. I want to leave it better. Making this county and Hollister safer will do that."

"That's an aspiration I can get behind." Ken nodded to himself. Leaving the county just a bit better than how he found it.

"Put that badge on and slap a magnetic sheriff's badge on your patrol vehicle, Sheriff Zorn. Congratulations, and let us know if you need help with anything related to Colby, manning, or pay."

"Thank you, sir, I will." Ken disconnected and rolled down his window. The fresh air slammed through his patrol vehicle, and he drew a deep breath.

Ken looked down at his speedometer and slowed as he approached a truck ahead of him. He saw a corner of a blue tarp in the back of the truck flipping in the wind. A finger of caution slid up his spine. He'd had enough dealings with people transporting stolen motorcycles through his county.

He picked up the radio. "Dot, this is Ken. Need you to run a plate for me."

"Sure, go ahead."

Ken gave her the North Dakota plate and drove behind the older model Ford while waiting for Dot to run the plate.

"It comes back to a 1990 Ford, black. No wants, no warrants." Dot's word eased that tickle of caution that had landed smack dab in the center of his gut.

"Roger that. Karen O'Dell will be in today. Give her access to anything she wants."

"I copy. Are you coming in?"

"Roger that after lunch. Do you need anything before that?"

"Negative. Just checking."

"See you soon." Ken passed the black Ford and took a long, hard look at the driver before he sped up and headed to Hollister.

* * *

Ken glanced at his watch. He needed to kill about a half hour before the diner would be full. He wouldn't repeat himself on the topic. He wanted maximum impact for the one time he would address it. He pulled into the Bit and Spur parking lot, ensuring his vehicle was out of sight from the town's main drag.

Declan's eyebrows shot up when he walked into the bar. "Ken. How you doing?"

"Had better days," Ken said as he sat on the barstool. "Can I get a Coke?"

"You got it." Declan poured him one over ice. "Hiding out?"

"Nope. Marking time. I'm only going to address what happened once. I'm waiting for the diner to fill up." He took a sip of his pop and sighed. "How're Mel and the boys?"

"Lordy, those two are the absolute best." Declan's smile was a mile wide. "And Mel is fantastic with them. I'm the luckiest man on Earth."

Ken smiled at his friend. "You deserve it."

"So do you. I heard your girlfriend told off

Allison the other morning." Declan poured himself a glass of iced tea and took a sip.

Ken shook his head. "See, that's just it. I finally found someone I like. Someone who understands and likes me for me, and Allison shows up out of the blue on my porch at dawn. Why in the hell would she do that, man? She's told me a million times there would never be anything between us. I moved on."

Declan leaned against the bar. "Dude, I don't understand women any better than you, but Mel and Gen were talking on the phone last night. It seems they believe Allison found out you were with someone and, right then and there, decided she needed to give you another chance. Not that I was trying to eavesdrop, but Mel was in the same room. Allison's embarrassed and wondering if she's screwed up."

Ken snorted. "Embarrassed, I get. But screwed up? More like she didn't want to lose her whipping post."

"That's what I figured, too. I think she always had you around, and that gave her a bit of power, you know. Now, she's got nothing," Declan agreed. "But Samantha is awesome, my friend. You keep hold of *that* woman."

As if he would let Sam go. In six months, she'd become his friend. In the last week, they'd made a huge jump to something better than he could have imagined, and damn it, it was worth the leap. Ken chuckled. "You have no idea. Last night, she waited for me at the Butte County Jail and told me not to drive back. I was an accident waiting to happen. I was so damn tired, and my mind was fried by what I was dealing with all day yesterday. She took me home, fed me, then gave me a couple of strong drinks and a massage. I fell asleep while she was working on my back."

Declan blinked and started to say something, then stopped. Ken frowned. "What?"

Declan shrugged. "Nothing, it's none of my business."

"Probably, but that's never stopped you before." Ken took a drink of his pop.

"Okay. It's just that we have a lot in common, you know. You've never had that before, have you? Me either. Before Mel, all I did was hook up. There was no relationship. But when you find someone who makes your heart explode open, you'd do anything to protect them … It's amazing and scary as shit. Makes all those others seem like they were just a waste of time."

Ken nodded. "You know I've dated. Nothing worked out. This kind of connection hasn't happened before Sam." Hell, some of the ones he dated had done more damage to his ego than Allison. They'd confused the hell out of him, to the point that he didn't have any faith in the fact that women liked him at all. Hell, it seemed like he was damned if he did and damned if he didn't. Damn. Ken sighed and rubbed his face. "I just hope she sticks around."

"Why wouldn't she?" Declan asked before he took a drink of his iced tea.

Ken lifted a shoulder. "I don't have the greatest track record."

"Doesn't mean shit if she's the right one for you. I wasn't expecting Mel or the babies, but it was right, and it was my future. You and Sam will figure it out." Declan slapped the bar top and laughed. "Ten bucks says she's already figured it out and is waiting for you to catch up."

Ken looked down at his drink, remembering her declaration the other day at the highway median. "Probably. I'm not the fastest on the uptake."

"Lord, join the club, my man. Join the club." Declan finished his tea. "Care if I go to the diner with you? No offense, but I have to know what went down yesterday. There are all kinds of rumors."

"Yeah, like what?" Ken said and then lifted his glass to finish his drink.

"Well, one was that Colby was running a sex ring."

Ken choked, and Coke came out of his nose. "Shit." He grabbed a napkin that was thrust in front of his face. Declan reached over the bar and hit him on the back. "Stop." Ken coughed and then tried to breathe. He blew his nose, but the pop acid had done a number on his sinuses. "Holy shit." He finally cleared his throat and was able to look up. "Warn a guy, will you?"

"Were they right?" Declan asked as he cleaned the counter.

"Hell, no."

Declan shrugged. "Would you tell me if they were?"

"No." Ken smiled at his friend.

Declan tossed the rag into a bin under the bar. "I'll grab my keys." He headed back to the office. "Other people said Colby was skimming from the payroll. People figured that was the only way he could afford to send his girls to those fancy colleges."

"What else?" Ken laughed but wasn't so sure those rumors wouldn't be substantiated.

"Drugs. He was transporting them for the cartel."

"Holy hell, we don't have a cartel." Ken shook his head.

"No one said we did; just said he was working for them." Declan tossed his keys in the air.

"Yeah, people have active imaginations." Ken moved to the door. "Want a ride?"

"I thought you'd never ask." They went outside, and Declan got into the passenger side of the patrol vehicle after locking up the Bit.

As they arrived at the café, they saw cars lining the street in front and a stream of people entering. "Wow, it's packed today. Wonder why?" Declan chuckled.

"Shut up," Ken grumped as he parked in front of Phil's garage, and they walked over. Ken took off his cowboy hat as he entered the diner. The place went silent.

"Ken. Saved a place for you." Alex and his fiancée Kayla were sitting at a booth.

"Thank you. Declan, have a seat. I'm going to kill the elephant in the room."

Declan clasped him on the shoulder. "Good luck."

Ken waited until Declan sat down. "As you all know, Colby was arrested yesterday. The pending charges against him are not for public debate."

"Why not? He works for us. We elected him. It's public record, isn't it?" Edna Michaelson asked.

Ken lifted his voice over hers. "The investigation is ongoing. There will be no public statements by this office until it's been cleared by the South Dakota Bureau of Investigations."

"What about Mable? She's not home. Is she okay?" Belinda Pratt, one of Edna's cronies, asked shyly from the corner.

Ken answered her question. "She will be. She's staying with her daughter until things are sorted out. Mable is not involved in any way."

"I want to know what's been done to make sure whatever it is that Colby has done won't happen again," Carson Schmidt said from the counter. "Edna's right. That information, the booking stuff, that's public."

"It is, Carson, it is. You can play private investigator and find out. I'm not stopping you. I am telling you that neither I nor anyone in my office will have any private or public comment about the charges." Ken put his hands on his hips.

Edna lifted her hand. "Excuse me? Your office? Has Colby been fired?"

"Relieved of duties until the allegations against him have been adjudicated. I was appointed interim sheriff by the governor."

Edna stood up. "Well, it's about time that idiot governor did something right." She walked up to Ken. "I appreciate your integrity, Ken. I'm glad you were picked. You're the man I'd want for sheriff." She grabbed his hand and shook it.

"I grieve that it had to happen this way, Edna, but thank you." The diner exploded with talk as people moved toward him and congratulated him.

Corrie rescued him. "Ken, I have your food. Everyone, let the man eat." She shooed people back to their seats.

Ken sat down with Alex, Kayla, and Declan. Kayla leaned closer to him. "These people go to bed way too early." She glanced around. "The Rapid station had a story on at the eleven o'clock news."

"Not everyone gets that channel with their satellite subscription, but it's in the digital version of the *Rapid City Journal*, too," Alex said. "Sorry you had to deal with that shit."

"What shit?" Declan pulled out his phone.

Ken sighed. "Thanks, but I can't talk about it."

"Never asked, did we?" Alex smiled at him.

"But I want to ask if the rumor about you and Sam is true?" Kayla bounced a bit in her seat beside her fiancé.

"Yeah, we're together." Ken smiled at Kayla. He felt his face heat, but damn it, he didn't care.

"Oh, shit." Declan scrolled as he said the word. "Fuck, man." He shook his head and put the phone down. "What in the hell?"

Ken shrugged. "I got no comment."

"And I can now understand that." Declan shook his head. "I have no appetite."

"I do," Ken said. Before digging into the beef stew, he took a piece of bread from the plate and slathered it in butter.

Alex drank his milk before asking, "Do you need help?"

Ken cocked his head. "As in?" He took a bite of his stew.

"I know a couple of guys who retired from the same profession I was in. They're looking for local law enforcement jobs. One has been through the academy."

Ken took another bite as he thought about the offer. "I don't know what the future will hold. I know Garth is okay doing full-time on a temporary basis. Give me the names and contact information. I can't say how long the investigation and adjudication will take, so it isn't anything that will happen soon if it does."

Alex nodded. "Just figured I'd ask. I'll write the info down for you, and you can pick it up when you finish lunch." Turning to Kayla, he asked, "Are you ready to go?"

"I am. I have so much work to do to prepare for the store opening on Saturday. Allison is over there right now working on her side of the building." Kayla scooted out of her seat, following Alex out of the diner. When Corrie cleared their plates, Ken pushed his food across the table and moved. Declan spread out and started to eat. "Thanks, man."

"No problem." Ken had been watching people finish and pay since he'd sat down. The diner was almost empty now. "What are you going to do with that information?"

"Not a damn thing." Declan looked across the

table at him. "People can find out on their own. I tell you what, though; he better not show his face around here again."

Ken snorted. "Don't make threats in front of an officer of the law."

Declan's eyes rose. "Oh, it wasn't a threat."

"Eat your food." Ken pointed at the stew. "Let me take care of the security of our community, okay?"

"Fine." Declan stabbed his spoon into his stew. "As a dad, that makes me sick."

"As someone who tries to be a decent human being ..." Ken shook his head. "So, what mischief are Jared and Scott getting up to?"

Declan caught the change in topic and dove into a story of his twins and Mel's adventure at Kinzer's dairy when Mel went to see if the Kinzers had a milk cow for sale.

"I thought you weren't into the ranching thing."

"I'm not, but let me tell you, those two can eat. We thought getting a milk cow was smart. Only now, I have to milk it. *Every* morning. As soon as the boys are old enough, they're taking over that chore."

Ken laughed with his friend and enjoyed the rest of his food. He paid for lunch and made his way back to Colby's office. Dot smiled when she saw him. The phone rang, and she answered it, holding up a finger. "Bridger County Sheriff's Office. Is this an emergency?" She rolled her eyes. "I'm sorry, I'm not at liberty to discuss any details. Do you have any other business with the sheriff's office? Ah huh? Okay, have a nice day." She hung up the phone. "It's been ringing off the hook."

"You're doing just as you should." Ken chuckled. "Where's Karen? I saw her truck outside."

"She's in Colby's office. The files she wanted were paper and in Colby's file cabinet. I took the key out of his desk. I hope that's okay?"

"Sure is. We don't have anything to hide."

"Unlike Colby." Dot shook her head. "Mable was horrified."

"We all were," Ken said. "I'm going to check on Karen. Have you had lunch?"

Dot smiled at him. "I have. I bring it so I can listen for the radio."

"Anything happening?"

"Just a thing up north. Garth called the game warden in. He stopped two guys with guns going into the wooded area just north of Trent Reeber's place. They claimed they were getting a jump on scouting things out for turkey season."

"Damn, that starts next weekend. Hell of a jump."

"Yeah, that's what Garth said. He's holding them until Dean shows up. Trent is there, so he's not alone."

"Good enough. I'll drive up after I check on Karen."

"Sounds good. Dean was up in North Dakota, so he's driving back."

"What was he doing up there?"

"Didn't ask." Dot chuckled. "Not my day to watch Dean."

Ken smiled and shook his head. "You're right. It isn't." He headed back into Colby's area and knocked on the door. Karen's head popped up, her eyes big behind her glasses.

"Hey, Ken. I'm glad you're here. I was going to ask Dot a question, but I'll ask you instead. I know I don't get out much, but who's Gary Ryan?"

"I've never heard of him. Why?" Ken walked in and sat down in the chair beside Colby's desk.

"He's been on the payroll as a deputy for the last four years." Karen turned the file around. "He makes more money than you do."

Ken leaned forward and stared at the payroll sheets. "Where's the check sent?"

Karen shook her head. "I don't know. I'll need to go to the county's payroll agency to find that out. You've never worked with this guy?"

"Karen, I've never heard of that person. As far as I know, he doesn't work for this department." Ken leaned back and yelled, "Dot, could you come here for a second?"

Dot appeared in the doorway a moment later. "What's up?"

"Do you know a Gary Ryan?"

Dot frowned and then blinked. "No. The only person I know of who has that name was Colby and Mable's son. He died from leukemia before they moved up here and Colby ran for office." Dot cocked her head. "Why?"

"Because Gary Ryan has been pulling a paycheck as a full-time deputy for the last four years," Karen O'Dell said, holding up a file as evidence.

Dot shook her head. "Nobody by that name works here."

"Okay, well, I need to alert the state about this irregularity." Karen sighed. "I was hoping it would be an easy audit."

"Do what you need to do, Karen. We want all

the irregularities found." Ken stood up. "Dot, whatever she needs, she gets."

"Yes, sir." Dot gave him a mock salute.

"Stop that. I'm heading out to check on Garth." Ken smiled despite the bad news Karen had dug up. He kept reminding himself it was Colby's mess, not his. Only the people of his county were the victims, and that ... well, that pissed him off.

CHAPTER 9

Sam slowed as she saw the sheriff's vehicle on the side of the road. She called out her position to her dispatcher and pulled behind the vehicle. A deputy raised his hand at her as she approached where they were located by the tree line. "Hey, need any help?" Sam said as she looked at two men sitting on the ground. Two high-powered rifles and several handguns were in a pile about fifty feet from the men.

"Hey, you must be Sam, the boss's ... ah ..." The deputy looked confused for a minute.

"Girlfriend?" Sam supplied.

"Right, I wasn't sure if that was the politically correct term. I'm Garth. J.D. the other deputy, is down south while Ken is handling stuff at the station."

"I've never been accused of being politically correct." Sam laughed and pointed at the two men sitting down. "What's up?"

"Ah, well, this is Trent Reeber, the landowner of this property."

Trent extended his hand toward her. "Pleasure."

"Nice to meet you." Sam smiled and shook his hand.

"Trent saw these guys, or maybe two others, last weekend. Saw them heading into the woods. I couldn't find them when I showed up. Today, I was driving by and saw a truck drop them off. The truck headed south, but I got them."

"What's their story?" Sam glanced at the rifles and handguns. "That's a lot of firepower."

"Said they were scoping out turkey hunting grounds. I had Dot run their IDs. Nothing came back on them, but I agree, that's a lot of firepower. If you used that rifle on a turkey, you wouldn't have anything left to eat."

"That's the truth," Sam agreed. It was suspicious, for sure. "So, are you citing them for trespassing?"

"I am, but I also called the game warden in. He's

going to do his thing. He can check to see if they have licenses. We have a big-time poaching problem during deer and antelope season, and as the price of meat goes up, I figured there would be an uptick every season." Garth shrugged. "They said their ride wouldn't be back until tonight sometime, so they have time to kill."

"Do they have ammo for the weapons?"

"Not the way you'd expect for going hunting. Maybe they were just checking the area out, but still, that's a lot of firepower." Garth nodded. "Two and two are not equaling four in this case."

"I don't like it. My boy and I work this land," Trent said. "They could have asked, but they sneaked into the woods. My ranch is right down the road. Not like they couldn't see it."

"Are there turkeys in there?" Sam asked.

"Some, not many this close to the road, but going back through that draw, there's land that the Hollisters own. We've ridden back there when the cows broke through the fence. Plenty of big boys back there." Trent shook his head. "The woods are thick as hell. It isn't an inviting place for people but a wildlife haven. The thing is, you can access it from the road about ten miles up that way. Why are they coming in this way?"

"Have you called the Hollisters to see if they've chased these guys out?" Sam asked Garth.

"Nope. But I think I'm going to do that now." Garth pointed to the two men he'd detained. "Keep an eye on those two for me?"

"Sure," Sam agreed. She shifted her attention to the men while talking to Trent. "Do you let people hunt on your land?"

"Sure, but I need to know people are out there. My boy's sixteen, and he's my world. I'm not going to let any nonhunting tourist with a gun on my land. But locals, they just need to tell me when they'll be out."

Sam nodded. "So, if Ken and I wanted to come out next weekend, with licenses, mind you, it would be okay?"

"Absolutely, but I'd call the Hollisters and ask them if you could hunt their land, too. As I said, that wooded area goes back a ways through the draw, and that's where most of the turkeys are." Trent lifted his chin toward the two men sitting on the ground. "What do you think they're talking about?"

"Wondering how much trouble they're in, no doubt." She glanced at the roadway and smiled as she saw Ken pull up behind her cruiser.

Trent chuckled. "Must be a slow day for law enforcement."

Sam laughed, too. "Major crimes up here, you know."

Ken talked with Garth, who handed him something. Ken looked at whatever the item was and spoke to Garth. Garth leaned closer to look at what he'd given Ken, and then Ken clasped Garth on the shoulder and spoke to him briefly before heading down to where they were. "Afternoon, Trent. Sam."

"Afternoon," Trent replied. Sam just smiled. The memories of that morning's sex pushed a blush to her cheeks.

Ken gave her that half smile before he turned to the men they'd detained. He handed their IDs to Sam. "See anything wrong with those?"

Sam looked at the IDs. She shifted them and snorted. "No holographic emblems, and they were issued after North Dakota established the design."

"What does that mean?" Trent asked.

Ken put his hands on his hips. "They're fake. I've got Garth calling down to Belle. We're arresting them and transporting them down to be booked and fingerprinted. We'll find out who they are. As to why they're here and the weapons, that will come later."

"Think they're stolen?" Trent asked. "The weapons, I mean?"

"I don't know. We'll be sure to track that down," Ken said. "Trooper Quinn, care to assist me?"

"Sharing the collar?" she asked jokingly as they moved toward the duo.

Ken shrugged. "If you want half the credit, it's yours."

Sam shook her head as they walked across the distance to the men. "No, sir. This is all down to Garth. He saw them getting out of the truck, detained them, and called it in. All I did was get us a good turkey hunting spot for next weekend."

Ken chuckled. "Good on you, trooper. Good on you."

"Was that a test?" Sam elbowed him.

"Nah, but it reinforced the fact that you're an amazing woman."

She smiled to herself as she walked with her man. God, that felt amazing to say. Her man. He was, wasn't he? And it was about damn time. She should have been more direct months ago. They stopped in front of the two men.

"Gentlemen," Ken said. "We seem to have a

problem. Your IDs are fake. Care to tell me who you really are?" They both glared up at him from where they sat, not speaking. "Well, that's okay. I'm reading you your rights. Trooper Quinn here will be my witness since I'm guessing you'll stay silent and won't acknowledge them."

Sam did one better than that. She initiated her body cam and got the advisement on film. They got the men up and did a thorough search instead of the safety pat down Garth had done when he'd initially detained them. The game warden pulled up by the time they had the men cuffed and searched and the weapons tagged and loaded in the back of Ken's vehicle.

Dean Burrows cocked his head as he approached. "Decide to take my poachers?" He extended his hand to Ken.

Ken clasped the game warden's hand. "Dean. Nope. Fake IDs coupled with trespassing. We're taking them down to get them printed and find out if we have criminals on our hands. They didn't have any other identification, so the line about turkey hunting was probably a ruse. Sorry to pull you away from what you were doing up north."

"Ah, hell, no worries. I'm trying to find a new camper shell for the back of my truck for deer and antelope season. Sleeping in the cab has gotten harder and harder these last few seasons." Dean turned to her. "Ma'am. I don't think we've met. I'm Dean Burrows, game warden around these parts."

"Samantha Quinn, I took over for—"

"Troy Flores. Knew Troy for years," Dean noted. "Welcome to the best-kept secret in the world. The people are awesome, and the country is still wild and beautiful."

"I'm sure loving it," Sam admitted. When she'd first moved, she thought the territory was empty and lonely, but it wasn't. The topography changed with the season. The land produced strong, independent people, and the land and its citizens had wormed their way into her heart.

Garth pulled away first, then Dean Burrows followed him. Trent had hoofed it back to his ranch across a pasture filled with Angus cattle. Ken leaned against his SUV. "The governor appointed me interim."

Sam glanced right and left before she toed up and kissed him. "Congratulations. You'll make a great sheriff." She was so happy and proud of him.

"Not happy about how it came to be, but thought maybe we might celebrate it tonight?" Ken dropped his hands to her hips. They felt so right there.

"How?" She lifted her eyebrows a couple of times.

He laughed. "Well, that, too, but how about we grill some steaks, fix a drink, and watch the sunset from the front porch first?"

"That sounds like heaven." Sam sighed.

"Did you bring that change of clothes?" Ken asked.

"I brought civies and two uniforms plus a small bathroom kit. I didn't want to be presumptuous …"

"You're not. If I could get you to move up and stay with me full-time, I'd be a happy camper." Ken shrugged. "But that's probably rushing things."

She cocked her head. "Maybe. And I have six months left on my lease in Belle."

"A target to shoot for, then." Ken dropped down and kissed her. It was quick but electric in how it zapped through her body.

"You're sounding like you're thinking long-term, sheriff."

"I am. Aren't you, trooper?"

She stared at him, completely serious. "I believe I am. However, I want to see how good of a hunter you are. Next weekend. Trent gave us permission to use this area, and I'll stop by the Hollisters' and ask permission to access their land from Trent's." Sam smiled when Ken's eyebrows shot up.

"I have to prove I'm good at hunting? Anything else I need to prove?"

Sam slowly shook her head from side to side. "Nope. You're a good person and a great lover, you sexy beast."

Ken's blush, as expected, was automatic. She laughed but continued, "You're a hell of a cop and can play chess. Hunting is the last box to tick. Oh, wait. Fishing. You can fish, right?"

"Of course." Ken scoffed.

"Good. Then, that's all that's on the list. What about your list? What do I have to prove?" She laughed the question, but Lord knew she wanted a straight answer.

He shook his head and gave her that half smile. "You've shown me who you are. You have nothing to prove as far as I'm concerned."

Sam sighed at the sincerity of his words and blinked fast a couple of times. "You kill me with your honesty, Ken."

"I'm only telling the truth." He was about to drop down for a kiss when her radio squawked with her call sign. He dropped his forehead to hers instead. "Go to work, trooper. I'll tell you my truth any time you want me to. See you tonight."

She nodded. "Tonight."

Sam moved to her car and got in. She answered her radio and pulled a U-turn, heading south to a semi that had run off the road the next county down. She glanced in the rearview mirror as she hit her lights and siren. Once again, Ken watched as she drove away. A smile spread across her face. It was nice to know someone was watching over her. She didn't need the protection, but his care and concern soaked through her with the warmth of one of his hugs.

CHAPTER 10

Sam glanced at the clock on the dashboard of her cruiser. The semi going off the road had been a mess. The driver was intoxicated, meaning she had a DUI to process. The truck took out about a mile of fence line, but the only damage beyond that was to the truck. The driver was unscathed and swore up and down that he had no idea how he drove off the road. Thankfully, the trailer was hauling an empty load. A tow truck had to be dispatched from Belle to get it out of the pasture it had landed in. Fortunately, no animals were grazing on the land. She called Ken on her way down to Belle with her drunk. She used the sobriety tests she'd administered on the scene to determine whether the man was under the influence of an intoxicating beverage. Not that the distinct odor of alcohol was ignored, but she was good at what she did. She had to get him to Belle and have blood drawn before he sobered up, but by how the man was staggering, she'd still have a legally drunk driver, even with the long drive down.

She processed her drunk and booked him into jail before heading north again. Even though she was off duty as of about thirty minutes ago, driving to where she'd stay for the night was authorized.

She pulled down Ken's drive and avoided several bigger potholes in the gravel road. He wasn't at his house when she arrived. She put the patrol vehicle into Park and pulled out her phone.

"Hey," Ken answered on the second ring.

"Hi, you. I'm at your house."

"There's a key under the big stone by the water spigot on the left side of the house. Go in and make yourself at home. I'll be about an hour. I have one stop in Hollister, and then, I'm on my way out."

"Okay. I'll probably shower and start seasoning those steaks with your extensive salt and pepper collection if that's okay."

Ken's laugh at her little joke was infectious. "Perfect. If you need anything for dinner, send me a text. I'll pick it up in Hollister before heading home."

Sam smiled at that. Home. She liked the sound of it. "I will. See you soon."

"Bye." Ken disconnected, and she went in search of the key. Once she found it, she opened the door, placed the key on the kitchen counter, and returned to her unit to grab her things. Then, she locked up the car and headed inside.

Ken's shower was just as massive as she remembered. The dual heads were a symphony of hot water that she could have relaxed in for hours, but she had a dinner to make. Sam dug into her duffle and donned a pair of shorts and a t-shirt before combing out her hair from the tight bun she wore for work. Having long hair was a liability, something a person she was arresting could use against her. The bun negated that liability. She took out the hairpins and unwound the long braid. Then she took the fastener out of the bottom of the plait and let the hair loose. Running her fingers through it from root to end, Sam flopped her hair over her shoulder and quickly brushed it. She should probably cut some of the length off, but she wasn't one to make an appointment to go to the beauty salon. The next time she went home, she'd have her mom cut off a foot or so.

She wandered up to the kitchen and snooped through the pantry and fridge. She used salt and pepper to season the steaks because Ken had no other spices except for the cinnamon she'd purchased the other night. She chuckled to herself and found the baking potatoes. She washed, oiled, salted, and pierced the big Idaho spuds before popping them into the oven. Ken had frozen veggies, but … she searched his pantry again. No bread. She foraged through the rest of the kitchen before texting Ken.

> Did you know you're out of bread?

> Yeah, I forgot about it. I was going to pick up some tomorrow. I'll grab a loaf.

> Get a loaf of something I can char on the grill.

> Done. Find everything else?

> Except for spices. We need to talk about that.

> LOL. Be there shortly.

Sam smiled, grabbed the OJ, and made herself a drink. She'd sit on the porch and wait for her man to come home.

* * *

Ken pulled up in front of Allison's bakery. The lights were on, and he could see her working in the kitchen. He parked his SUV and made his way into the little shop.

"Just a minute," Allison called from the back when the bells over the door sounded. "I'm not open, but I do have some ... Oh. Hi." She stopped where she was but continued to wipe her hands. "What do you want?"

"Bread," Ken said and walked farther into the shop. "A couple of loaves, please."

"Sourdough, buckwheat, rye, or white?" Allison asked, turning away from him.

"A loaf of sourdough and white." He moved up to the counter and pulled out his wallet. "How are you?" he asked as politely as he could.

"Mortified. Thanks for asking." Allison pulled a bag out and slid a round loaf into it. The sourdough, he presumed.

"About?" Ken asked as she put the loaf on the counter.

"Did you come in here to rub it in?" Allison put her hands on her hips.

"No. But you don't need to be embarrassed. Samantha and I both understand what was happening and why."

Allison snorted and went to the other display

case. "Then tell me what was going on because I'm damn sure I lost my ever-loving mind."

Ken waited until she came back with the loaf of white bread. "You got worried I wasn't going to be around anymore. You've been mad at me for so long that it startled you when you discovered I'd moved on. You didn't want to lose the familiarity of us, even though it was toxic."

Allison blinked at him and then moved to the register. "That sounds like Doc Wheeler talking."

"No, just an observation from this side of the fence." Ken shrugged. "We've been done for a long time. Any hopes of anything other than friendship is gone."

"Friends? Why in the hell would you want to be friends with me?" Allison threw her hands up in the air.

"Because we're adults with a shared past who live in a small town. I can continue the way we've been, but it takes a lot of energy that I don't want to invest." Ken sighed. "Carrying hatred in your heart has to be exhausting for you, too."

Allison pushed both loaves of bread toward him. "Leave. Please." Ken reached for his wallet, but she interrupted him. "Take it. Just leave, I don't want your money." Allison's jaw locked down, and her face turned red.

"I can't do that." He dropped a ten-dollar bill on the counter and picked up his bread. "Goodbye, Allison."

Ken took the bread and walked out of the door. He turned back and caught Allison breaking down in tears. "Damn it."

He walked back into the store, put the bread on the counter, went around it, and pulled Allison into his arms as she sobbed, "I don't hate you. I never have. I just …"

"It's okay." He held her gently as she continued to cry. When she could control herself, she pushed away, and he let her go. He grabbed a napkin off the counter, handing it to her.

"Thanks." Allison wiped her face and blew her nose. "I'm okay."

"I know." Ken stepped back. "You always have been."

Allison snorted. "My folks said I was being stupid and that I'd lost you for good."

Ken gave her a half smile. "That happened a long time before Samantha showed up."

"Yeah, I know." Allison took a shaking breath in

and then blew it out slowly. "I'm sorry for the bitch I've been."

"Apology accepted." Ken shoved his hands into his pockets. "I wish you all the best. You'll find a guy who treats you how you deserve to be treated."

"Right." Allison snorted. "Here in Hollister? I don't think so."

"You never know. Look at the couples around here. New people always show up, and who knows, maybe someone from around here is into you. I was for a long time."

Allison gave him a quick, barely-there smile. "Thanks."

"I'm heading home. Thank you for your time and the bread." Ken walked around the counter as he spoke.

"You don't have to pay," Allison said again.

"I do. I'm interim sheriff, and I don't want any room for allegations on my behavior."

"Congratulations on your appointment," Allison said when he reached for the bread.

"Thanks. I'd rather it hadn't happened this way, but ..." Ken headed to the door.

"Ken?" Allison called after him, and he turned back. "I hope you and Samantha are happy. She could have come off as a total bitch when I showed up, but she didn't."

"I heard the conversation." Ken nodded. "Thank you. I'll see you around." He lifted a hand and went out the door.

When he got into his vehicle, a weight around his shoulders that had been hanging there for years slipped off and shattered into fragments. Closure was a good thing for him and Allison. He pulled out and headed toward the highway and his way home.

As he pulled into his driveway, his headlights illuminated the back of Sam's patrol vehicle. A smile spread across his face at the sight of warm, yellow light spilling out of the windows of his home.

He parked and grabbed the bread before locking his vehicle. She stood up from the rocking chair where she'd been sitting, welcoming him with a smile. "Welcome home."

Ken bent down and kissed her. "Best greeting in the world." He lifted the two loaves of bread. "I wasn't sure what kind to get. One sourdough and one white."

"I was expecting sliced bread in a plastic sleeve. Where did you get this?"

"Allison's bakery. She isn't open until tomorrow, but I knew she'd have something."

"Oh, this looks fantastic." Sam took out the round loaf. "We'll use this. How did talking to her go?"

"I made her cry." Ken removed his hat and put it on the peg by the door.

Sam's head whipped around. "What?"

"I explained that it was too much of an energy suck to deal with her the way things had been, and I told her she had to be exhausted hating me for as long as she had. She told me to leave. I dropped a ten on the counter for the bread and walked out. I looked back, and she was crying."

"And ..." Sam slid the bread knife out of the butcher's block.

Ken narrowed his eyes at her. "What do you mean 'and'?"

"Oh, come on. I've known you for over six months. You went back in. What happened?"

Ken crossed his arms over his chest and leaned back on the counter. "I held her while she cried, and when she got ahold of herself, I stepped back and gave her a napkin. She was a mess."

Sam cut a piece of bread off the loaf and turned around. She pulled off a piece and put it in her mouth. "Oh, man. So good," she said. "I'm still waiting for the rest of the story."

"She apologized and told me you were decent to her the day she came here. She said you could have been a bitch, but you weren't." Ken smiled at her. "I told her she'd be okay and that, sooner or later, the right person would show up for her."

Sam smiled at him. "You are the sweetest man on the face of the earth."

Ken rolled his eyes. "I'm going to go take a shower, then start the grill."

"The potatoes are in the oven, so grilling can start anytime." Sam linked her arm with his and walked back to the bedroom. "What happened in the world of Colby today?"

Ken groaned. He'd almost been able to forget about Colby for a minute. "It would appear he's been skimming funds. There was a person on the payroll who had never worked a day at the station. Full-time and getting paid more than I was. Turns out the name on the paycheck was the same as Colby's deceased son's name."

Sam took his gun belt when he unfastened it and put it beside hers in the bedroom. "Do they know how much money he embezzled?"

"I didn't ask." Ken pulled his uniform shirt out

of his pants and unfastened it after he removed his badge.

Sam took his badge and put it on the dresser beside hers. "Any word about an arraignment?"

"Yeah, it'll be next Friday. The grand jury convenes on Thursday. I called Senior and told him he needed to call the district attorney and let him know what the county auditor found. I don't know if those charges will make it onto the docket, but the South Dakota Bureau of Investigations got a warrant and is scrubbing his bank accounts."

"Sounds like they're on top of this one. Doesn't it usually take months to make it to the grand jury?"

"I think the governor has this on a fast track. He campaigned on cleaning up the system, getting rid of corrupt people."

"That's true. I didn't think about that. Has the news of what happened made the rounds yet?"

"Yeah, the story broke in the *Rapid Journal*. Alex and Kayla knew about it when I went to the diner at lunch." Ken stripped out of his pants and briefs, then put the uniform in the dirty clothes hamper and walked into the bathroom.

"You have the best ass."

Ken jerked and looked back at Sam. "What?"

"What, what?" she asked. "Can't a woman admire the view?" She leaned against the door frame and let her eyes slowly travel down and then back up again. "Delicious."

His cock twitched at the look she was giving him. "You could come into the shower with me. Grilling can wait, right?"

Her shirt was off before he finished his suggestion. He laughed and turned on the shower. She shed her shorts and panties and walked across the room as Ken ducked under the water. He held out his hand and watched her walk to him. *How in the hell did I get so lucky?*

CHAPTER 11

Ken sat outside the grand jury's chamber. Makala Dennis, the agent who conducted the investigation, was in with the grand jury. He would be testifying before Dot.

"I've never testified before," Dot said again.

"I know. You just tell the truth and answer their questions to the best of your ability." He patted her arm, reassuring her yet again. The assistant district attorney sitting with them looked up from his case files and smiled at her but didn't say anything before returning to his work.

"Sheriff, we're ready for you." The ADA in charge of the grand jury came into the small room.

Ken followed him into the chamber, and the foreperson approached him.

"Sheriff, raise your right hand and repeat after me," the ADA said. Ken took the oath and then sat in the witness box. The grand jury was spread around the chamber. "Sheriff, introduce yourself to us and tell the jury about your law enforcement experience."

"I'm Ken Zorn. I've been a deputy in Bridger County for fifteen years."

"Thank you. Could you tell us in your own words the events that transpired concerning the case before us now?"

Ken nodded and spoke, telling the jury his actions from the time he walked into the station. He focused on being direct and concise.

When he finished, one of the jury members asked, "Did you see what was on his computer?"

"The picture? Yes, sir. It was a young girl. She was naked."

"Do you know how young?" a woman asked.

"I have a friend with teenage girls. She wasn't that old but wasn't a baby either." Ken shook his head. "Under ten."

"And the photographs you found? How many were there?" another asked.

"A box of them. I didn't count, but more than twenty," Ken replied.

"Do you know what was on the sheriff's computer?" someone else asked.

"No, sir, I do not. Investigator Dennis should know."

"As to the embezzlement charge. There's no such person working for the department, correct?" That came from the foreperson.

"No, sir. As I said, I've worked for the department for fifteen years. It's small; there are five of us, and until recently, there were only three. That person has never worked with or for us."

After a lull in the conversation, the ADA stood up. "Any other questions?" Silence was his answer. "Thank you. You're dismissed."

Ken got up and exited the way he'd come. He sat down with Dot. "It didn't hurt a bit."

Dot swatted sweetly at him and laughed. He pulled out his phone when she was called in and texted Sam.

> Done. Taking Dot to lunch after, and then we will head north.

> Copy. Spending the night in Belle. Will bring rifles, ammo, and an orange vest up and be at your house before dawn.

KEN SMILED. He hadn't been so excited to go turkey hunting in eons.

Dot was in and out of the grand jury room quickly. After having lunch, they headed back to Hollister, where Ken dropped Dot off and circled back to take a cruise through the small town. When he pulled into Phil's garage for gas, Phil came out and shook his hand. "Heard you got a promotion."

Ken shook his friend's hand. "Temporary, for now."

Phil inserted the fuel nozzle into the SUV's gas tank. "Read the article from the *Journal* the other day. Colby sure as hell isn't welcome around here."

Ken rubbed the back of his neck. "I can't talk about it, Phil."

"I know it. We all do. But we can talk, and we aren't spreading rumors. Going by the facts in the paper, he's being held for child pornography. He shows his face around here, he won't get a warm welcome. We're family people up here. Hell, my girls ..." Phil shook his head. "I trusted that bastard. I voted for him. Makes me sick to my stomach."

"I understand how you feel. It's valid, but remember, he's innocent until proven guilty. That's how America works." Ken knew the man was guilty, but justice had to be served—and not vigilante justice. Taking matters into your own hands was as lawless as the crimes committed.

Phil didn't answer and watched the dial spin on the gas pump. "Can I ask you a question?"

"Sure." Ken leaned against his SUV.

"Would you let him near your family, your girls, if you had them?"

Ken studied the toe of his boot. "No. Can't say as I would."

"That's what I thought. I'm not saying squat to anyone around here. I can keep my mouth shut, you know I can, but this situation, let me tell you, has shocked a lot of people. We've been talking, and we want you to run for sheriff when the time comes."

Ken's head jerked up. "That could be months, if

not years, depending on how long Colby's attorneys can prolong the trial."

"Don't care. Just thought you should know," Phil said as he pulled the nozzle out of the tank. "I'll put this on the county's bill."

"Thank you. I'm going to hit the diner for a soda. Want one?"

Phil looked at his watch. "Nope, I have an hour and a half before I go have my beer at the Bit. Don't want to spoil my thirst."

"See you later." Ken got into his SUV and pulled it into a parking spot at the diner, clearing the pump area for anyone needing fuel. He made his way into the diner and sat down at the counter.

Gen Hollister peeked out of the kitchen pass-through window. "Hey, Ken. Soda?"

"Yes, ma'am, please." He smiled at her. Coming from the south, Gen called pop soda, which took a hot minute for his brain to translate when she first started up the diner.

Andrew Hollister came out of the kitchen with a plate. "Want some brownies? Corrie made some. Her son, Barry, is coming into town, and she's making some of his favorites. She bribed me to leave with these."

Ken took one of the warm chocolate creations and took a bite. "Damn, these are good."

"Right?" Andrew chuckled. Gen came out of the kitchen with his pop, and Ken smiled at the size of her belly.

"When are you due?" he asked. She set his pop in front of him and put her hands on her back, grimacing. "Almost a week ago."

"We came in today to schedule her C-Section. Zeke called down for us. If that young man doesn't show up by this time next week, he'll be born in Belle." Andrew stood up. "You should probably get off your feet."

He pulled a chair from one of the tables for her to sit on. "Thank you." Gen put her hands on top of her belly. "How are things going with you?"

"Busy. Learning the ropes. Dot is good about cracking the whip when I need to sign paperwork. There isn't much more to it." Ken shrugged and took a sip of his Coke.

"You should be the sheriff. We always call you, not your dispatch or Colby, when we need help." Gen started to rub her belly. "You've been here through thick and thin."

"This is my home. Wouldn't be anywhere else."

He let the comment about him being sheriff slide without answering it.

"As I said." Gen chuckled. "How's Mable doing? Have you heard from her?"

Ken shook his head. "Not since she left. Dot may be in contact with her." He probably needed to give her a call and check on her, and he would when he heard whether or not the grand jury had indicted Colby.

"I want to do something nice for her. She's a victim, too." Gen sighed. "Drew, help me up, please. Your son is bouncing on my bladder again."

Andrew was up before Ken could even register the request. He helped her out of the chair and watched her waddle back through the kitchen. "I have no idea how she does it." Andrew sat down beside Ken again and grabbed another brownie. "I'll be a piece of mush on the floor when she delivers. I can't stand for her to be hurt or in pain."

"What?" Ken stopped as he was reaching for another brownie.

"Dude, she made me watch Lamaze videos. They had real women giving birth." Andrew closed his eyes and shook his head. "I've seen any number of animals give birth, but damn, what a woman goes through …" He looked over at Ken. "They say women are the fairer sex, but to go through childbirth, they're fucking battle-tested warriors. Make no mistake about it." And with that visual, Ken decided against the second brownie. Andrew chuckled and took the brownie Ken was about to grab. "You'll see. Wait until you start your family."

Ken's mind instantly flashed to Samantha. It was way too soon to talk about children. Way too soon, and she was a career woman, so he wasn't sure she'd even want a family. He did, but his desires couldn't usurp hers. "That's a long way off." Andrew took another brownie. "Is that your third?" Ken chuckled.

"Fifth. I have sympathy cravings." Andrew shrugged and bit into the brownie. "And these are fucking amazing."

Ken picked up the last brownie on the plate. "Yeah, they are."

"Andrew!" Corrie's scared voice called from the back of the building.

Ken was up and following Andrew through the kitchen. Corrie was beside the bathroom door. "What's wrong?" Andrew asked as he pushed the door open, revealing Gen on the toilet.

"I think my water broke."

"Are you having contractions?"

"No. Is the baby going to be okay?"

"Absolutely, this happens all the time," Ken said from behind Andrew. The biggest thing was to keep Gen calm and get her to a doctor. Ken wasn't about to let her freak out. "Andrew, let's get her to the clinic." He turned to Corrie. "Please call Zeke and tell him we're on our way over."

Andrew helped her stand and pulled her maternity pants back up while Ken pretended to be interested in something in the other direction.

"I'm too heavy for you to carry," Gen protested when Andrew bent down to pick her up.

"You'll never be that heavy," Andrew said. "Hang on to my neck, babe. We're heading out of here."

Ken went ahead of Andrew and opened the door. He walked with Andrew across the street and up about two hundred yards. Zeke met them at the door, and Andrew followed him into the exam room.

Stephanie leaned against the door to her office and spoke when the exam room door shut. "I have coffee if you're going to wait around."

Ken smiled at her. Thank God they'd worked out their issues. His history with Stephanie was spotted with misinformation and misplaced judgment. He'd slapped himself pretty hard when he realized he was judging Stephanie in the same way Allison had been judging him. He'd pulled his head out of his ass and apologized to her.

"Thank you. I'll stay until I know if they need to be transported to Belle. I can legally go over the speed limit, and I'd rather take them to meet the ambulance than have Andrew drive."

"True. Would you rather have a pop or water?" Steph said as they moved into her office. "Water, please." He sat down and took the cup of water she offered him.

"What's all the noise about?" Doc Wheeler popped into the office.

"Gen. Her water broke, I think," Ken said as he stood and shook his hand.

Jeremiah looked at Stephanie. "Did you call Eden?" Jeremiah's wife, Eden Wheeler, was a nurse practitioner and midwife.

Stephanie nodded. "I did. She's getting the kids together, and she'll be here shortly. I can watch them if you have patients coming in."

"We don't pay you to be our babysitter, Steph." Jeremiah smiled at the woman.

"I don't want payment. I want this clinic to run

smoothly and for healthy babies to be delivered." She smiled at both of them.

"Well, thank you. I have one appointment coming up from Rapid. I could cancel, but he's probably almost here." Jeremiah glanced at his watch and then the exam room door. "My sister picked the perfect time to go into labor, didn't she?"

"I don't think she had much say in it." Stephanie laughed. "Take your time. I have coloring books and crafts we can make. We'll spread out in the lobby and make glitter bombs."

Ken's eyes went wide. "What?"

Stephanie laughed. "That's what Eden calls my crafts. We put glue on paper and then sprinkle glitter on the glue. Somehow, it always falls off."

"In the van, in the house, in the shower. I've even found it on my tractor, and God only knows how that happened." Jeremiah chuckled. A chime of bells from the back of the building floated toward them. "If you're sure, Steph?"

She waved him out of the office. "I've got this. You do your thing."

"Thank you. I owe you a raise," Jeremiah said as he walked down the hall.

"I'll take you up on that!" she called after him and laughed. "I love this town."

Ken nodded. "I do, too."

"Then you should run for sheriff," Steph said, sipping her drink.

"You're like the third or fourth person to say that today."

"Then you better start listening. It's the universe telling you to pay attention." They visited for about ten minutes before Steph's eyes went to the door across the hall. Zeke came out. "Is Eden on her way?"

"Yep," Stephanie said. "Do you need the ambulance?"

"No. They're comfortable with delivering here. The baby's head is down, and she's dilated to a six. Andrew wanted to know if you'd call Senior and let him know."

"I can do that," Ken said and stood up as Eden Wheeler, her son, and her daughter jogged into the clinic.

"I'm here. Steph, is Jeremiah busy?"

"He is. I'm watching the kids," Steph said, motioning for the kids to come into her office.

"I'll call Senior and see myself out," Ken said to

no one in particular. He dialed the number to the ranch.

Senior answered after five rings. "Hollister."

"Senior, this is Ken Zorn."

"What's wrong?"

Ken smiled. It was an expected response when he called. "Nothing, sir, but you might want to come into the clinic. Gen is in labor."

"Hot damn. It's about time. Do they need anything?"

"No, sir, not that I know of." Ken chuckled.

"I'll be in straight away."

Ken disconnected and pocketed his phone. He headed back to the diner to make sure Corrie knew what was happening, then went to the station, where he signed that week's timecards, which Dot now kept, and certified them based on the sheets she presented to him, which the deputies were now required to fill out and sign.

"Anything else?" Ken asked her as she hesitated in front of his desk.

"Yeah. Ken, I've been thinking long and hard about it. I think, no, I *know* I want to give you my notice. I'm closer to seventy than I am sixty. And this situation with Colby has just tipped the scales in favor of retiring."

"Damn, Dot. I can't imagine this office without you at that desk." He nodded in the direction of her guard post to Colby's office.

"I'm sure you can find someone to run the office more efficiently. I'll hang around and train them. I'm not leaving you in a lurch. You've got a lot of things up in the air. Just start looking around. I'd like to be retired come the first of the year, so you've got time." Dot sighed. "I'm just tired, Ken. For the longest time, I thought what he was doing was the best for everyone, and finding out what he was actually doing ... I'm just done."

"I can understand your feelings, Dot. I'll put the word out, and you start spreading it, too. The office will move into Hollister instead of out here in the middle of nowhere. Senior is building us a new one."

"Well, then, it's a good thing I'm retiring. Driving another twenty-five minutes to Hollister isn't my idea of fun." Dot chuckled, adding, "Especially in the snow."

"I get it." Ken chuckled with her. He glanced at his watch. "I'm going back to Hollister to check in on Gen."

"Call me and let me know when she has the baby."

"I will. Night, Dot."

"Night, Ken."

Ken got into his patrol vehicle and dialed Sam.

"Hello, this is Trooper Quinn. How may I assist you, Sheriff Zorn?"

Ken put the phone on hands-free and pulled out of the parking lot. "I'm heading down to Hollister and thought I'd call to make sure you couldn't be persuaded to come up tonight." He smiled as he heard her sexy laugh.

"You know I can be, but it'll be late. We have a district meeting tonight, and I still need to pack."

Ken shook his head. "Then don't drive up. I was being selfish." He wanted her in his bed. Hell, he wanted her in his life full-time.

"Believe me, I thought about it, but I can grab five or six hours, drive up, and still be ready to go hunting. Oh, crap."

He tensed immediately. "What?"

"I never went to the Hollisters' to ask them if we could hunt in that draw behind Trent Reeber's place."

"I can do that. Gen Hollister is in labor, and Senior is at the clinic. I was going to go check on them."

"It's about time. Wasn't she due a couple of weeks ago or something?" Sam asked.

"A week ago. I was at the diner having a Coke when she went into labor. Oh, and Corrie made some brownies that were out of this world."

"Now, I'm hungry." Sam chuckled.

"I'll see if I can nab a couple for hunting tomorrow."

"Oh, yes, pah-leese!" Sam begged. "We'll expend enough calories."

Ken snorted, "Yeah, I was worried about that."

"Oh, hush, Mr. Metabolism." She laughed, and the sound filled his SUV.

"I'll see you in the morning," Ken said.

"I wish I was sleeping next to you tonight."

"So do I, but I want you to be safe."

"Another reason I think you're the best, Sheriff Zorn."

They talked until he arrived at the clinic in Hollister. He said goodbye as he pulled up and parked. He opened the door to the lobby and stopped. A glitter bomb was right. Piles of red, green, blue, purple, and gold glitter were mounded on pieces of paper. The floor was lined with them.

Ken tiptoed through the art projects and found Senior in the office. "Ken." He took a sip of his coffee and pointed to the pot. "Come to sit vigil with me?"

"Not exactly." Ken chuckled. "Sam and I got permission from Trent Reeber to hunt turkeys in his tree claim, but he said the best hunting is farther west down the draw that you own. Would you have any problem with us hunting there?"

"Son, that isn't my land. That's the Bureau of Land Management's asset. I have a lease with them, which is probably why Trent thought it was mine. My cattle aren't anywhere near that area and won't be until wintertime. I'll let Rusty know you'll be out there, but you should be alone."

"I appreciate it. I'll drop a turkey or two off at the diner if we get our limit. Hoping to spread the wealth."

"You're a good man." Ken cringed when he heard Gen scream in the other room, and Senior paled. "Damn," the older man whispered.

"She's strong, sir." Ken clasped him on the shoulder.

An infant's wail came out of the exam room shortly after. "There you go." Ken was relieved to hear the baby's cry.

Senior nodded. "Need to make sure Gen's okay,

too." The man took a breath. "She has to be. Andrew needs her. We need her."

Ken understood Senior's concern. He'd raised Andrew by himself. He'd been stricter than hell with his son and drove a wedge between them. Only when Andrew was discharged from the Marines did the two of them work out their issues.

About five minutes later, Andrew opened the door and came out. "They're both fine. Gen wanted me to come out and tell you. She knew you'd be worried."

Senior sagged with relief. "That's good. I was."

"Eden is going to do some things with Gen and the baby, but she said to tell you it'll be about a half hour, maybe a little more, then you can come in and see for yourself."

"Thank you, son. Go be with your family. I'll be here waiting." Senior smiled at his son.

Andrew was through the door in the next second.

"Congratulations, Senior. Do you know what they named him?"

"Andrew Hollister the Seventh. Gen says they are going to call him Sev for short. Short for Seven. What a thought." Senior laughed. "I wouldn't put it past her to do just that."

Ken laughed at the thought, but Sev had a ring to it. It wouldn't be bad, and the kid would be loved, that was for sure.

"Do you need to get out of here?" Senior asked. Something in the strain on the man's face led Ken to believe he needed company.

"No, sir, I don't have a better place to be right now. Is that coffee fresh?"

Senior nodded. "Stephanie made it before she took the kids back to Jeremiah's area."

"Then how about I join you for a cup until you get to go in and be a grandpa."

Senior's face split into a wide smile. "Grandpa. Damned if I don't like that name."

"You'll be one of the best, sir." Ken poured a cup of coffee he probably wouldn't drink and sat down with Senior. The man needed someone to talk to, and he had nowhere to be until zero dark thirty tomorrow morning.

CHAPTER 12

Sam laughed at Ken. He was covered in feathers but still plucking away. She put down the plastic garbage bags and collected the overflowing feathers from the box they'd started using. Four turkeys in one day was a darn good haul. They were all long beards or older Toms averaging about twenty-five to thirty pounds each —massive birds.

Ken was cleaning the last turkey. She'd soaked each of the ones he'd plucked to clean out the cavities and then poured a bit of hot water on the skin to tighten it and make the pin feathers that had broken when they were being plucked stand out. She used a needle nose, pulled them out, and retrieved any stray buckshot from the bird. She cut up the three turkeys they'd already processed and bagged them, putting them into the freezer. They'd put the last bird into the fridge after she cleaned it, then take it to the diner. Corrie and Ciera would use it to keep the price of the meals down. Sam had never thought about it, but with the abundance of wildlife in the area, sharing the hunt made sense.

"Almost done," Ken said as he worked on the last wing of the big bird. He handed it to her, and she took it into the kitchen to finish the work. By the time she was done, Ken was inside and had cleaned up. She washed and accepted a beer. Then they walked out onto the porch and sat down. "That was a good day." She sighed and started the rocker moving.

"I really enjoyed it. Although, you missed the last one."

She pushed him a bit. "Not true. You missed."

"Beg to disagree." Ken laughed and took a sip of his beer.

"Are we going to have to have a shoot-off, sheriff?"

Ken chuckled. "Probably. I shot it."

"No, I did." She was adamant that she'd hit the bird.

"If you say so," Ken said.

She snickered. "I'm so whooping your ass on the shooting range."

"If you say so," Ken repeated and took a drink of his beer. Sam laughed hard until she heard Ken's phone ring. She got quiet fast and listened as he answered, "Zorn."

Sam couldn't hear the speaker at the end of the connection, but she saw Ken's eyes dart to hers. "Why me?" The person on the other end spoke, and Ken closed his eyes. "When?"

"Yeah, I'll be there." He hung up the phone. "Colby is the gift that keeps on giving."

"What happened?"

"He got a lawyer, and the lawyer wants to cut a deal. The Bureau of Investigations wants me down at the jail tomorrow by one. He says the BOI wouldn't believe what he's offering without me to confirm his information."

"What in the hell could you possibly validate?" Sam turned in the rocker facing him.

"I have no idea. Whatever it is, I hope he doesn't get out of the charges." Ken's jaw cranked tight. "No one would let that happen."

Sam sat back in the rocker. *Yeah, they would.* She'd interned at the DA's office in Vermillion when she was at law school there. The DA would always go after the bigger fish. The consensus was the little fish would fuck up again, and sooner or later, they'd be caught. But she'd never seen anyone bargain with a case like Colby's. Those types of charges stuck and stuck hard.

"They might reduce the charges," she finally said.

"How could they?" Ken shook his head.

She explained her time in the DA's office and what she'd witnessed about bigger fish. "But that's putting the horse way before the cart. We don't know what he has to offer, and until the DA does, they won't strike a deal. Will he talk without a guarantee?"

Ken shook his head. "No, he won't. He's too cagey."

Sam nodded. "Makes you wonder what could be worse than what he's charged with."

* * *

Ken shook the hand of the man who would be in the jail interview room with him. "I'm Mitchell Farmer, and this is Derek Meyers. Glad you could make it."

Ken nodded. "Wasn't given much of a choice."

Mitchell sighed. "Yeah, I get that. He called this meeting, and his lawyer mentioned you specifically. We're going to listen to what he has to offer."

"What does he want in return for this important information?" Ken put air quotes around important.

"The child porn charges dropped," Mitchell said.

Ken jacked forward in the chair he'd just sat down in. "What? You can't. Have you seen—"

Mitchell held up his hand. "I have. I get it. His attorney will frame the information, so you'll understand what the man has, but he won't give us the key information until a deal is struck."

"What if I don't know what the hell he's talking about?" Ken almost hoped he didn't. Colby getting out of any of the charges would be wrong.

Mitchell nodded. "Then, at this time, the DA's office is not inclined to drop any charges." Mitchell looked at his watch. "Please excuse me for a minute. I have to step out and make a call. I'll be right back."

Mitchell walked out, and the man introduced as Derek Meyers cleared his throat. "Listen, Mitchell can't say it, and as the DA, he *wouldn't*, but I'm going to. This asshole isn't going to get a deal.

The DA's office has to act in good faith, so they'll listen to him, but you and I know the magnitude of his crimes is such that he has to have the location of Capone's vault before he gets anyone to listen. So, from me to you, listen to what Colby says. If you can run with the information he does give us, it would be all the better. Play dumb. Ask questions that will clarify things in your mind. Make him mad so he'll slip up. Take what he'll give us. When we leave, you can tell me what you think. If you have any suspicions, investigate what he's given you, and in the meantime, we'll put him away. Ask all the questions you can. If his lawyer permits the guy to talk, let him talk. He's full of himself and thinks he can beat these charges. Don't let him do it."

"I can do that," Ken agreed. Not more than two minutes later, Mitchell and another man walked in. "Ken, this is Clive Dugan, Mr. Reicher's attorney. Mr. Reicher is on his way down."

Ken nodded to the attorney but kept his mouth shut. Colby's lawyer unbuttoned his suit jacket and sat down. He stared directly at Ken for a long moment before looking at the door impatiently. The man's suit was nice, and his shirt was bright white and pressed well. Ken figured it cost Colby and Mable money for this representation.

The door opened, and a deputy brought Colby in. He was handcuffed and shackled.

"Do you need shackles? He isn't a violent offender," Colby's lawyer drawled.

"Policy." The deputy looked at the DA. "I'll be right outside the door."

"Thank you." The DA sat down across from Clive and Colby. "We're here at your request. The floor is yours."

"I want a guarantee that the charges will be dropped before I say a word." Colby almost yelled the words. "I can't do time as a cop *and* be convicted on those charges." His attorney put his hand on Colby's arm reassuringly. The move looked practiced, and Ken sneered a bit in his mind. How had he ever looked up to that man?

Mitchell sighed, "That's something you should have thought about before committing the crime. We're done here." Mitchell and Derek stood up, and Ken followed suit.

"I'm sure we can come to an agreement," Clive said, stilling all of them.

Mitchell turned around. "I want enough information to prove this is worth entertaining, and I won't be yelled at again." The man stared at Colby.

"Of course." Clive patted Colby's arm. "Tell them what you told me."

Ken leaned against the wall. He was farther away from Colby, which was fine by him.

"A national car theft ring is using my county as a staging area." Colby leaned forward to look at Ken. "Right under your nose."

Ken snorted. "Right. Because there's so much traffic through the county."

Colby sneered at him. "At night," the man snarled.

"Sure." Ken rolled his eyes.

Colby leaned forward even more. "You couldn't find them if you tried. I got them hidden. They've been paying me. You and that damn mechanic almost fucked that up last winter."

Clive's head snapped toward Colby. "That's enough."

"No, it isn't. You want me to believe a criminal syndicate is operating in *my* county?" Ken scoffed.

"It's my county!" Colby stood up.

"Not anymore," Ken stated flatly.

"They chop up the cars and the motorcycles and ship the parts out via Highway 85, and they transport them to the coast on I-94 east and west. You're such a fucking idiot, Zorn. You can't see what's happening in front of your face. Why the hell do you think I hired you? Because you're stupid."

Ken moved away from the wall. "I don't believe you, Colby. You're trying to wiggle out of the crimes you committed. There isn't any place something like that could be done. I know these ranchers. They'd notice."

"Not if it isn't private property," Colby shot back.

"Enough!" Clive shouted, and Colby looked at him. "Enough," Clive repeated.

Ken stared at Colby. *So, on government land. That narrows the search down.*

Colby sat down, and Mitchell looked over at him. "Sheriff Zorn, what do you think?"

"I think he's lying. He hasn't given us anything other than desperate claims." Holy hell, it took everything he had in him not to run out of that room and head north to find those people.

"We can prove the payments and will give you the location of the staging area," Clive said.

Ken snorted, but Mitchell held up a hand. "And you would want what in return?"

"As I said, all child pornography charges are to be dropped. We're talking about a multi-million-dollar operation here, Mitchell. It would be the conviction of a lifetime for a small-town ADA like yourself."

Mitchell stared at the table, and his thumb bounced up and down on the surface as he thought. "I'll present your offering to the DA. I'll let you know what she says, but I will recommend she decline."

Colby growled and leaned forward to look at Ken again. "You tell Marshall if I don't get this deal, I'll spill everything."

Ken made a face. "I have no idea what you're talking about. I think he's lost it."

"I'll tell the press! I'll tell everyone. You tell him!" Colby raged. The deputy outside opened the door and roared, "Sit down!" Colby snarled and made a move toward Ken, but the deputy dropped him into the chair.

"Counselor, I'll let you know what the DA says." Mitchell had to shout over Colby as the three of them took their leave.

They walked down the hall as Colby's ranting and yelling followed them. As soon as they were out of earshot, Mitchell stopped. "Sheriff, I'm sorry we wasted your time. If you ever need anything from us, just let us know."

"Thank you, sir." Ken dipped his head.

Mitchell frowned. "Do you know what he was talking about at the end? Who's Marshall?"

"Sir, I can honestly say I don't know anyone by the first name of Marshall. The rest of it sounded bizarre, didn't it?"

"It did. Derek, you ready?"

"I'll be in a minute. I need to visit with the sheriff for a moment."

Mitchell nodded. "I'll meet you at the exit."

Derek smiled, and they waited for Mitchell to get out of earshot. "Did you get enough?"

"Yeah. They're on government land if they aren't on private property. The Bureau of Land Management has a lot of acres up there, but it narrows the search."

"And this Marshall person?"

Ken shook his head. "That's something I don't understand."

Derek narrowed his eyes, then nodded. "Find these guys, sheriff."

"I will." He'd find them and get them out of his county.

They exited the jail, and Ken shook Mitchell

and Derek's hand before he got back in his SUV and headed north. As soon as he was on Highway 85 heading north, he called Frank Marshall.

"Mr. Marshall, I was down in Belle today. Colby was trying to exchange information to eliminate his child pornography charges. It got dicey, and at the very end, he threatened to tell the press everything he knew about you."

Frank Marshall was silent for a long moment. "Thank you for the call, Ken. We're good. You don't worry yourself about any of his nonsense. Do your job and take care of the county. I can take care of my interests."

"All right, sir. By the way, would you know where I could find night vision goggles?"

Frank grunted. "Think I do. How many pairs would you need?"

"Two," Ken replied.

"Stop by the house. They'll be waiting for you."

"Thank you, sir. I'm on my way from Belle." Ken disconnected and then tried to remember every piece of BLM land in the county. There would be quite a few sleepless nights in his future, but it would be worth it if he could get those guys.

CHAPTER 13

Sam sat on Ken's front porch with a glass of iced tea and soaked in the nature surrounding her. The quietness of the place soothed something deep inside. The house and, of course, Ken were a balm to her soul. Her phone vibrated where it sat beside her. She smiled at the number displayed. "Hi, Mom."

"Are you working?" Her mother always asked the same question. She was married to a trooper and understood the job.

"I wouldn't answer if I was busy. I'm sitting on a beautiful front porch listening to the birds sing and drinking an iced tea."

"That sounds wonderful. Where? Your apartment doesn't have a porch."

"I'm at Ken's," she answered with a smile.

"Your deputy?" Her mom rushed the question.

"Yes, my deputy."

"What? When did this happen? You have to tell me everything!" Her mom rattled off the questions.

"Well, about a month ago, maybe a bit less, we were working together running radar."

"That's code for talking and bullshitting," her mom quipped.

"Maybe," Sam conceded. "Anyway, I got frustrated—"

"No, not you."

"Mom, do you want me to tell you this?" Sam looked heavenward.

"I'm sorry. My lips are sealed. Go ahead." Her mom's laughter didn't give Sam any confidence that she was telling the truth, but she dived into what had happened and their time together since.

"So, is he as perfect as you thought he was now that you know him better?"

Sam sighed. "Mom, he's better than perfect. A genuinely nice person who cares so much about this community."

"And sexy."

Sam snorted a laugh. "He is, but I'm not going there with you."

Her mom's throaty laugh filled her ears. "I don't blame you. Have you talked about a future together?"

"He mentioned something about me living with him. I told him I had a lease." She looked down at her jeans and shrugged. "Besides, with our careers, it could be hard for me to travel from here without a place to stay at Belle."

Her mom was silent for a moment. "You know there's a remedy to that."

Sam sighed. That again. "Mom..."

"No, before you shut down, just listen for a minute with an open mind."

Sam tried not to smile, but she knew what her mom would say and, she'd already halfway decided she would move in that direction anyway. "Okay. My mind is open."

"If you study and take the bar, you can get a stipend from the state to practice up there. I was researching it online. Underserved counties qualify for a five-year allowance, like the one Hollister is in. Granted, it isn't much, but it would help put groceries on the table until you built up your practice. Plus, you wouldn't have to worry about patrolling and could start a family."

Sam blinked at that last comment. "Do you

already have me married to Ken in your head?" Sam had recently let her mind travel that road, but her mom was quick with those thoughts.

Her mom made a sound that sounded a bit like she was deciding. "Well, *maybe*, but if the relationship gets more serious, it's a way to maximize your time together. Growing up as a trooper's kid, you know that Dad's schedule was based on the whims of the supervisors. There will be weeks when you're required to cover some other area and won't see him."

"I'm aware," Sam admitted. Sergeant Stapleton, her district supervisor, had threatened to pull her down south to cover manning shortages in the more populated areas. "And, for the first time, I'm willing to admit, that's not a bad idea."

"What? What did you say? Could you please repeat that?" her mom asked hurriedly. "Wait, I'm putting you on speaker. Your dad needs to hear this."

Sam laughed, the same throaty laugh as her mom. "All right, all right. I admit that the idea of taking the bar and settling down here has merit. I've been thinking about it lately." Since she and Ken had gotten serious, it had been in her thoughts frequently. A law career provided stability.

As her mom spoke to her dad, "Hallelujah" came across the connection.

Sam shook her head. "I'm not saying I'll do it, but it's a viable option." She'd even looked at where she could take the bar and when the next test was scheduled.

"We'll take it," her dad said. "You know I don't want you on the road. We both know how dangerous it is."

"We do." She was willing to admit it. While working as a trooper, several of her fellow officers had been injured while on duty. Thankfully, none had been killed, but across the nation, troopers fell in the line of duty, and Sergeant Stapleton made sure they knew the circumstances so they could hopefully avoid the same situation. "Hey, Dad, I went turkey hunting yesterday."

Sam successfully changed the topic and visited with her parents for about forty-five minutes before they hung up. She loved them for the support and gentle prodding they gave her now that she was out of the house. Her law degree was a requirement her father mandated before she became a trooper. She enjoyed her studies, and being a lawyer wouldn't be a bad career, but she'd been laser-focused on being a trooper for as long as she could remember. She had an academy class waiting for her a month after she graduated. Had she thought twice about becoming a trooper after graduating with honors from law school? Yes. More than twice, but she'd committed to the academy, and it had been her lifelong dream to become a state trooper. And if she'd gone into law, she would never have met Ken or been introduced to that wonderful community, so she didn't regret her decision. But now, well, she'd see where Ken wanted to go with the relationship. There were options if they wanted them.

The sound of tires on the gravel road brought her from her musings. She got up and walked to the stairs as Ken's SUV came down the road. She walked to his door and, when he got out, said, "Hi, stranger. How did it go?" The look on Ken's face was more than enough answer. "What?" She let him pull her into a hug. Looking up at him when he released her, her stomach dropped to somewhere around her knees. "They didn't do a deal with him, did they?"

"Not that I'm aware of. He was trying to trade information on a vehicle theft ring that he said was national in scope. He made a slip and said it wasn't on private property and was operating right under my nose."

"That doesn't make any sense." Sam frowned. "Unless it's on government land?"

"Bingo," Ken said as they walked into the house. "There are acres and acres of Bureau of Land Management parcels up here." Ken opened the fridge and took out the pitcher of iced tea. He poured a glass. "He also said they were moving at night."

"So, we stake out the roads during the night." Sam crossed her arms.

"The problem is that if they see a patrol or sheriff's vehicle, we might scare them off. Plus, Colby being arrested has made the news. If these people are halfway intelligent, they'd move the operation if they're no longer protected." Ken took a long drink. "I've acquired two sets of night vision goggles. I plan to do some recon tomorrow and then narrow it down tomorrow night."

"I'm in," Sam said immediately.

"You'd need approval from your district supervisor. Otherwise, you might not be covered by insurance and such."

Sam knew what he was saying was true, but …

She looked up at him and smiled. "I can get approval. It'll cost me, but…"

Ken set the glass down. "What will it cost you, exactly?"

"I can get my dad to authorize it." She was sure he'd agree if she baited the hook correctly.

Ken crossed his arms over his chest. "Again, what exactly will it cost you?"

Sam waved him off. "Nothing I can't pay. I'm in. We start tomorrow?"

"There are a few hours of daylight left today. I want to call Dean Burrows and have him help me identify all the government land on a map. He knows the back parts of this county better than anyone. He's walked it a million times."

"The game warden, right?"

"Yep. I know the roads and the ranches; Dean knows the land beyond the ranches better than I do."

"All right, you call him, and I'll make my phone call. I'll be right back." Ken narrowed his eyes at her.

She toed up and kissed him. "Don't worry. It's nothing illegal or immoral. I wouldn't do that, and you know it."

He dropped his hands to her hips. "I do, but I don't want you to make any sacrifices."

"Hardly a sacrifice." She hoped. But she would bite the bullet.

"I'm going to go change and give him a call, but don't burn any bridges because of me."

"You're worth every bridge I've ever crossed." She got a wicked kiss for that comment and was left breathless as she watched Ken go to the back of the house. Samantha stepped outside, walked down the gravel road, and placed her call.

"Hello?"

"Hey, Dad."

"Why are you calling me on my work cell?" His confusion was obvious.

"Because this involves work." She told him about the information Colby had given Ken.

"You'd need to clear that through Stapleton. It's his district." Her father said exactly what she knew to be true.

"I'd like to bypass him and get permission from you. He won't approve it. Manning is at an all-time low, and he's threatening to move me down south as it is. His opinion is that a woman trooper shouldn't be this far from assistance."

"Yeah, well, nobody said he wasn't an ass," her father agreed.

"Dad, here's the deal. If you do this for me, get me this permission and coverage, I'll study for the bar and take it."

Her father was silent for a moment. "And quit?"

She'd anticipated that question. "I need a minimum of six months to study. I'll schedule the bar for after the first of the year. Regardless of whether I pass, I'll give my two weeks' notice after I get the results." She huffed out a laugh. "If things don't work out between Ken and me, I'm moving back home until I can find a job, though."

Her dad was silent again. "I won't make you quit if you don't pass. I don't know if I've ever told you this, but before you went to the academy, I had a dream about you. You were in a trooper's uniform. You were shot." He cleared his voice. "It was bad. I've never forgotten it. I need you to be safe, Sammie. No matter what happens. You need to be safe."

Sam blinked the tears from her own eyes. Her mom had told her about it. Her father didn't sleep for days after that happened. She hated that she was the cause of his distress, but she was bullheaded and stubborn and hell-bent on becoming a trooper back then. "Dad, I'm a damn good cop, but there are always risks, you know that. You should have told me about this a long time ago."

"Would it have changed your mind?" he asked.

"At that time, probably not. But that's water under a bridge I crossed long ago." She was honest with him. "I've been doing this job for three years, but I can't see doing it for the rest of my life. And thanks to my mom and dad, I have something to fall back on. This case is very important for Ken. He's going to run for sheriff when Colby is convicted. Having this case in his back pocket will ensure he's elected."

"It wouldn't hurt, that's for sure. What about the others in his department?"

"One full-time deputy besides Ken and two part-timers with very little practical experience. One of them missed identifying a couple of fake IDs without holographs."

She heard her father sigh. "I'll work it. Stapleton will have a cow, but I've delivered a few heifers from him before. Have your sheriff shoot me an email tonight requesting assistance."

"We'll do it right away. Thanks, Dad."

"I'm holding you to taking the bar exam. Please

be careful, Sammie." Her dad used the name he called her when she was young.

"Always, Dad. Always." She hung up the phone and jogged back toward the house. Maybe she'd made a rash decision, but it felt right, and she'd learned from her dad to go with her gut. Tonight, her gut told her that she and Ken were together for the long haul, and her future wasn't with the troopers.

CHAPTER 14

Ken looked across the table at Dean Burrows, J.D., his counterpart in the northern part of the county, and Garth. Sam was sitting beside him. He left Douglas, their other temporary hire, on patrol and directed him to stay in the middle part of the county until notified. He wasn't leaving his county unprotected.

"Now that we're all here, I'll tell you what's happening."

J.D. chuckled. "You mean it wasn't to drink iced tea and bullshit?" He glanced at Sam. "Begging your pardon, ma'am."

Sam smiled at him. "Thank you, but being raised by a trooper and working with them for the last three years, I've become slightly immune to crass words."

J.D. shrugged. "Regardless, my mom would tan my hide if she heard me speak like that in front of a lady."

"Anyway," Ken said, interrupting the conversation. "I went down to Belle today. Colby was trying to make a deal to get out of the child porn charges."

"No way!" J.D. stood up. "I got kids, Ken. That can't happen."

"Relax. I got a call from the DA when you were driving down. They declined the plea deal. *But …*" He glanced at each of them. "Colby gave me some information. Information I think we can use to find and stop the transportation of stolen vehicles and motorcycles. Colby says they're using Bridger County as a staging area."

"Nah, the ranchers would have told us if something like that was happening," Garth said.

"He's right," J.D. agreed.

"Not necessarily." Dean shook his head. "What if they took up residence on government land? Ones without current leases."

"Bingo," Ken said as he pulled out a county map. "I know some of the government land, but not all of it."

"Hold on. I have a map in my truck." Dean got up and trotted out to his vehicle.

"What else did that son of a—" J.D. looked at Sam and changed his words. "—gun say?"

Dean came back in and dropped a map on the table. "He said Alex and I almost ruined this money-making enterprise for him last year. Remember the accident with the tow truck and the stolen bike?"

"Yeah. That could've been so much worse." Garth rubbed the back of his neck. "Dang, good thing Alex has military training."

"It was," Ken agreed.

"Money-making? Is Colby getting a cut of this?" Dean asked.

"From what I could gather, he's getting paid to keep us away from them. Have you ever had Colby tell you not to go to a specific place?" Ken glanced at the three across from him.

Everyone shook their head. "He didn't talk to me," Dean said.

"Nope," J.D. said.

"Never," Garth replied.

Ken thought for a moment. "All right. Get out your phones and take a picture of Dean's map. We're going to attack this in two ways.

"First, tomorrow night, I want all of us to find places to park along 85 in our privately owned vehicles. Somewhere unobtrusive. I want to monitor traffic. J.D., you're up here." Ken pointed to the northern border of Bridger County. "Garth, you're on the southern border. Every time a vehicle comes in or goes out of the county, you call it into all of us."

"Why?" Garth asked.

"Colby said they were coming in at night. We've all been up all day today. Work your schedules so you can grab some sleep tomorrow during the day. Find a shade tree, turn up your radio, and get some rest."

"Dang. I like this job. Getting paid to sleep." Garth chuckled.

"I set my schedule," Dean said. "I'll make sure I'm ready."

"Good. Sam and I will take these two locations. The Bit is a great place to park. I'll let Declan know I'll be there, but not why. He's good about keeping his mouth shut." Ken would explain it all to him when he was able. "Each time the vehicle passes us, we'll chime in."

J.D. leaned forward. "Because if it doesn't pass

us, we'll have a tighter location for where to search."

"Exactly," Sam said. "Then, we all converge on the location and start the search when the sun comes up. We don't want headlights to give us away."

Ken nodded. He'd run his plan by Sam before the guys had arrived. "And with Dean's knowledge of the government land, we can move in as a team and circle them."

"Are they armed?"

"I'm thinking yes." Ken leaned back. "Those two you stopped the other day near Trent's. They were packing. I have a strong suspicion they're somewhere around Trent's place, but we worked the area yesterday when we were hunting turkeys, and we didn't see or hear anything."

"What was the final disposition on those two?" J.D. asked.

"Canadian residents. The guns were ghost guns," Garth said. "I sighted them for trespassing, and Butte County notified the proper authorities. As far as I know, they're gone."

"Ghost guns. Man, people are buying the parts and pieces off the internet and putting them together. I can see the challenge of building a weapon from the ground up, but bad people can do wicked things with them."

"They can," Ken agreed. "Thank God our people are responsible gun owners, for the most part."

"What happens if there's no traffic tomorrow night?" J.D. asked.

"We'll do it again the next night." Ken leaned forward. "The five of us have to work together. We're at their mercy if we stumble on this place without backup. But the five of us working together, that's a force that these city slickers don't want to mess with."

"So, no snooping around tomorrow?" Dean asked.

Ken shook his head. "You're a hell of a game warden, Dean. I'd like to keep you alive. If this is the multi-million-dollar industry Colby said it was, these people will want to protect what they're doing, and killing a country bumpkin or two probably wouldn't bother the people who are getting rich."

Dean stared at Ken for a surprised second. "Yeah, okay. Alive is not overrated."

"It is not." Ken sat back. "Okay, pictures of the

map and rest up tomorrow. It could be a long night."

"You got it." The men pulled out their phones and snapped pictures of Dean's map.

Ken dropped his arm over Samantha's shoulders as they drove away. "You think it'll work?" He hoped like hell he wasn't making a mess.

"I do. I believe you're right. They have to be somewhere along that draw, but we tramped all over it."

Ken shook his head. "Some of it. You saw the map. It meanders and then hooks back toward the road. A hell of a lot of acreage we didn't cover and a couple of good size buttes in between."

"Will five of us be enough?"

Ken shook his head. "No, but I know someone who may be able to even the odds a bit."

"Who?"

"A mechanic who I hear is one hell of a shot."

Sam frowned. "Alex?"

"Yep."

"You'll have to fill me in. He's a good shot?"

"One of the best." Ken sighed and looked down at her. "There's still time to back out."

Sam shook her head. "Nope. I've set the ball in motion, and there's no stopping it."

"Are you going to tell me the price you're paying for helping me?"

Sam nodded to the rocker and bench. "Let's have a seat."

"That sounds serious," Ken said as they made their way over to their seats.

"I told you that I graduated from law school in Vermillion before I joined the state patrol, right?"

Ken nodded. She'd mentioned it several times through the months they'd known each other. "Yeah. Your dad insisted you have a fallback plan."

"Well, I'm falling back."

Ken snapped his head in her direction. "You're quitting?"

Sam waggled her hand in the air. "Kind of. I told my dad that if he got me through this operation with you, I'd study and take the bar."

Ken swallowed hard. A vise twisted in his chest, but he gutted through and asked, "What does that mean for us?"

Sam turned toward him and put her hand on his thigh. "I want this to work between us. I know the sex part is new and fabulous, but we were friends before we got involved."

Ken stood up. "You want us to be friends?" Fuck, that was a kick in the nuts.

"No, I mean, yes." Sam stood up and grabbed his arm. "I want to practice law here in Hollister. I know it wouldn't bring in much money, but if you're elected sheriff, it would be enough, right?"

Ken turned toward her and tried deciphering what she was saying. "Sam, you gotta be a bit clearer here."

She turned away and then spun back. "I think I'm in love with you, Ken. I want to live with you and maybe someday marry you. I don't want to be on patrol, and I think that while there isn't a huge need for a—"

Ken stepped forward, pulled her into his arms, and dropped his lips over hers. *God, yes. Yes to everything she said.* He kissed her as if it were his last moment on earth. When he finally lifted away from her, she sighed and leaned into him.

"I'm taking it. I didn't make a mistake by telling my dad I'd take the bar?"

"No. You didn't." Ken held her. "Break your lease. Move up here. You can study out here, where there are no distractions. I want you here. I need you in my life, and yes to everything you said. Live with me. Marry me."

Sam arched her back to look up at him. "I want to. God, yes, I will, but we need to take this a step at a time. I was planning on working while I studied."

He pulled her into him and held her as tightly as he could. He felt invincible and terrified at the same time. He could provide for both of them. "I don't make much money but have enough for both of us. Well, unless you want to buy another gold-plated Desert Eagle. I tend to have to budget for those types of things."

Sam held him as tightly as he was holding her. "We haven't even said we love each other."

Ken released his hold and looked down at her. "Samantha, make no mistake about it; I am in love with you. I've been a little bit in love with you since the day you rolled up on that tow truck accident, and it's been growing day by day. I know I'm clueless about what to do between us sometimes …"

Sam's eyebrow raised in a sexy arch. "Sometimes?"

Ken barked out a laugh. "Okay, all right, I admit it; I'm clueless all the time, but I love you. Remember that when I'm being particularly dense, will you?"

A slow smile spread across her face. "I love you, too. You'll have to remember that when I'm too abrupt, or I do things without letting you know what I'm doing. Like taking the bar."

"Give your two weeks' notice after we catch these guys." Ken dropped a light kiss on her lips.

Sam shook her head. "That's not fair to you. I wouldn't be able to help with the bills or anything."

"There are no bills other than electricity. I own this land, thanks to my parents. My truck is ancient and paid off. There isn't a mortgage on the house, and I didn't go into debt when I put the addition on. You'd be able to study without interruption. Break your lease. I'll help you pay whatever the cost is to break it. Put in your notice. Live with me, and someday, when it's time, we'll get married." Ken swallowed hard. He'd put it all out there for her. It wasn't pretty, but it was his truth.

She stared at him for longer than was comfortable, but he kept eye contact. Finally, she nodded. "All right. I'll move in and marry you when the time is right."

"And put in your notice?" He wanted her there with him full-time, not hit-and-miss.

"After we get this bust, I'll put in my notice. If you're sure."

"Why don't I take you back to the bedroom and show you how sure I am?" Ken pushed his hips forward. Sam moved against him. "You may have to show me more than once."

Ken dropped down and flipped her over his shoulder.

"Ken, you have to stop doing this. I'm too heavy."

"Never." He swatted her ass, and she yelped and then laughed. His chest swelled when all the emotion he hadn't named and had tried desperately not to acknowledge filled him to overflowing. He'd found the person he'd fight like hell to protect and die for. Declan was right. It was like nothing he'd ever had, and he'd fight with his last breath to keep those feelings.

CHAPTER 15

Ken listened to his radio as another truck was identified coming south. It was three in the morning, and his coffee thermos was empty. So far, the transient vehicles had traveled right on through the county.

"Hey, Ken, I got a big truck heading north. It looks like an old moving truck." Dean's voice shattered the silence in his vehicle.

"Copy. Garth, let me know."

"Roger."

"The truck J.D. saw just passed me," Sam said. "Red Chevy."

"Copy," Ken said from his tucked-away corner by the bar. He looked toward the north on Highway 85. Five minutes later, headlights showed up on the horizon. Ken waited for the truck to pass him. "Red Chevy heading your way, Garth."

"Copy. The moving truck just passed me. It's moving slow, about fifty-five or so. Won't be to you for a while if it keeps going at that speed."

"Understood," Ken said, shifting in his seat. He waited for ten minutes and heard the red truck clear Garth's location. Finally, the moving truck trundled through the intersection that led into Hollister. "Moving truck heading your way, Sam."

"Copy," she said. "I'm getting out and doing some jumping jacks."

"Oh, damn. Good Idea," Garth said.

Ken chuckled. "Just be back in the truck before the moving truck gets there."

"I said I was doing some jumping jacks, not running a marathon." Sam laughed. "It took forever to get to you."

"You got told, Ken." Dean chuckled.

"That I did, Dean. That I did." Ken laughed. They were tired and punch drunk because of it, but they worked through it.

Ken got out of his truck and stretched, too. Hollister was all buttoned up. The little town was growing, but it was still a village more than a town. He took a breath and looked up at the stars in the heavens. Of all the places to be in this world, he couldn't think of a better place to live and raise a family.

He got back into the truck and got comfortable. Time passed quietly and slowly. Finally, he glanced at his watch. "Anything yet, Sam?"

"Just broke the horizon," she said.

"Is someone pushing it?" J.D. asked with a laugh.

"Seems like it," Sam answered. About five minutes later, she said, "Past me and heading your way, J.D."

"Copy."

"Anyone want to play I Spy?" Garth came across the radio about ten minutes later.

"No."

"No, thanks."

"Don't think so."

Ken laughed as the replies came back.

"Fine, I'm going to do more jumping jacks." The man sounded like he was pouting, and it was hilarious. Ken laughed again and settled back to wait. After fifteen minutes, he keyed the mic. "J.D.? You got anything."

"No, sir. Nothing. Darker than sin, and no headlights anywhere," J.D. responded.

"Roger. Keep an eye out. We may have our area."

"About where I found those guys," Garth said.

"That's a twenty-five-mile stretch between them, but yeah, I think it's that area."

"Ballsy of Colby to put them that close to the Hollisters' ranch," Dean said. "But smart, too."

"That's the truth," Ken agreed. Thirty minutes later, he called J.D.

"J.D., come in toward Hollister and see if that truck broke down between you and Sam."

"Roger," J.D. acknowledged.

Sam broke the silence next. "I have headlights."

"That's me," J.D. replied. "There were no breakdowns on the road."

"All right. Each of you get some sleep. We'll meet at Trent Reeber's place tomorrow morning at eight. That way, all the kids have been picked up from bus stops, and everyone going to work at Hollister or Buffalo is through the area." They acknowledged his words. He waited for Sam's SUV to pass his location before falling in behind her. It took another fifteen minutes to get back to his house.

She stretched as he got out of his truck. "I'm

too old to do this." She yawned, which caused him to yawn.

"You're younger than me. Come on. Food, then sleep," he said through his yawn and dropped his arm around her shoulders.

"I'm not hungry." She yawned again. "Sleep."

"All right." He shut and locked the door behind them. He took off his gun belt, and so did she. They put them beside each other in the bedroom. He stripped down, and so did she, but she went to his dresser, pulled out one of his old t-shirts, and slipped it on. He pulled her into him, and she fell asleep within minutes. As tired as he was, his mind was whirling with what he needed to do in the morning.

The first thing would be a warrant to look for the ring on state land. They had reasonable belief that a crime was being committed, and they'd narrowed the scope of the area, so hopefully, Ken could get the judge to sign off on it. A few other matters trickled through his thoughts until Colby's words once again echoed through his mind. *You're such a fucking idiot, Zorn. You can't see what's happening in front of your face. Why the hell do you think I hired you? Because you're stupid."*

He tried damn hard not to let the words sting. But

they'd burrowed deep in his hide, and they were festering. He knew he wasn't the brightest bulb in the basket regarding women. Thank God Samantha wasn't a wallflower and spoke her mind, or he'd never have had that, what was between them, in his life.

However, when it came to caring for the people of that county, he knew one thing for certain. *He was damn good at his job*. Damn good, and that son of a bitch Colby would soon learn that lesson.

* * *

TRENT REEBER EXITED the barn as all their vehicles converged at the ranch house. He walked out of the structure with his son, who was the same height as him. "Ken? Is there a problem?"

"No, no. Everything is fine. I hope you don't mind, but we'd like to use your place as a staging area. We think there might be some undesirables back past your land."

"Back where you hunted turkey?" Brantley asked.

"Past that a bit," Ken said.

"You're welcome to stage here. Do you need any help?"

"No, but we're waiting for two more."

"Well, I can put a pot of coffee on," Trent said.

"Thanks, but you two do whatever you need to do. We're going to wait for the others and then head out. I appreciate you letting us meet up here and maybe leave a vehicle or two."

"Not a problem. Brantley, let's head back and finish up in the barn."

"Deputy Zorn, are you sure you don't want coffee?" Brantley asked. "I'm over mucking out the stalls."

Ken laughed and shook his head. "Sorry, son. We won't be here that long."

Trent reached up and rustled Brantley's hair. "Trying to duck out of work."

Brantley bent and jogged ahead of his dad. "No, just trying to postpone it."

Ken waited until they were out of earshot. "Dean, I've been studying this map but don't know the land. Where would you be able to drive a truck of that size without raising suspicion?"

Dean leaned over the map and pointed. "I'd say here, but Senior has a lease on this property. His cows and his hands would be all over it."

"No, he doesn't," Sam said. "I mean, he doesn't

have cows on the land. Right?" She looked up at Ken.

"That's what he told me when Gen was having her baby." Ken nodded. "Where in here?"

The sound of a pickup coming down the drive turned all heads. Alex Thompson pulled up and got out of the truck. "Ken. I brought my spotter with me. This is Brian; he goes by Nail."

"We've met several times." Ken stretched out his hand. "This is Trooper Samantha Quinn, my deputies, Garth and J.D., and this is Dean Burrows, our game warden. I woke up Judge Chain at dawn. He was a bit grumpy but said he'd sign the warrant for this property." Ken made eye contact with Alex and Nail. "You two understand you'll be non-players on the takedown, right? When I signal, I want you to kick up a dust and make them think we have more people than we do. Could be all for naught, but I'm not taking any chances."

"We got it. We'll make them think a world of hurt is raining down on them." Nail chuckled.

"That will work, but you don't shoot anyone. I don't have the pull or the intelligence to get you out of that charge."

Alex leveled a hard gaze at him. "I only hit the shit I aim at, sheriff."

"All right. We believe our varmints are holed up in this area." Both Nail and Alex looked down at the map. "Dean, you were about to tell us where you'd set up if you knew no one was going to be around here."

"This is an old homestead. It has to be at least two hundred years old, but it's in a natural valley. It has a well. I've stopped there a couple of times over the years. There's a farmhouse that's in real sad shape. The barns, however, were built to last." Dean pulled a pen from his shirt pocket. "Here." He turned the map over. "This is the valley. Here's the road leading into it. The turn-in is about five miles past Hollisters' main gate. Look for the blue reflector and turn in. Go through the cattle gate and hold to the fence line. You'll see another cattle gate about two miles or so farther in. Use it and follow the road to the homestead." He drew the route in. "The barns are here and here. The house is here, and this is the well house."

"What's the quickest route here?" Nail turned the map back around and pointed to the rise above the homestead.

"Same way, but instead of turning down the road to the homestead, you'd go about another mile and then straight up the side of the butte that forms the rise," Dean said.

Alex sighed. "It'll take me a hot minute to climb that rise, Ken. I can do it, but it'll take time. This leg isn't what it used to be."

"You take all the time you need. Garth and J.D., I want you to come up the back way." He trailed his fingers along the route he and Sam had taken while hunting. "Circle back up this way, over the ridge, and down the slope. You take up positions here and here." Ken looked at his men.

J.D. bumped Alex with his elbow. "Take your time. It'll take us a while to get through this area. And make sure you watch us come down that ridge, so we don't get skinned by one of your bullets."

"Hell, J.D., you took the fun out of the day." Alex laughed.

"What do you want me to do?" Dean asked.

"I need you to block the road. Here." Ken looked at him. "Nobody comes out. Take out the vehicles, but don't kill anyone."

Dean frowned. "I'm with Alex. I don't shoot stuff I don't aim at."

"Not intending to offend anyone," Ken said to soothe the ruffled feathers.

"When everyone is in position, Sam and I will drive in and block the way out with our vehicles here." He pointed to the map Dean had drawn. He glanced at Sam, who nodded her understanding.

"We'll need a radio," Alex said.

"Here. Channel One. Dot is listening in case we need medical." Ken handed them his radio. "Does everyone understand?" Ken got head shakes all around. "All right. Let's get these guys."

CHAPTER 16

Sam waited with Ken as the men worked up to their positions. Dean had gone back to block off the access point, so no one came in behind them.

She glanced over at Ken. "Alex said 'spotter'. So, were they a sniper team?"

Ken nodded. "I didn't know he'd have to climb that thing."

"His leg?" Sam asked. He'd mentioned it wasn't what it used to be.

"Yeah, he had a bad accident, and his leg is held together with nuts and bolts. His words, not mine." Ken sighed and stared at the high rise of the butte.

"His friend can help him get where he needs to go, right?" She hoped so. It would be tough going, but having a sniper to dust things up, as Ken said, would be helpful.

"Probably." Ken shook his head. "Hope I don't get people killed."

"Hey." Sam waited until he looked at her. "You have planned this to the last degree. There's nothing that can be done about the hill. If Alex can't make it, we'll deal. There's nothing that can be done if these criminals get stupid."

"You be careful when we're in there," Ken said, staring at her intently.

"I will be if you are," she replied.

"That's a deal."

"Ken, we're in position, watching J.D. and Garth come down the slope." Alex's words rang through the cabin of his SUV.

"Slope? Hell, this is a fucking one-hundred-and-eighty-degree drop," Garth whispered on the radio.

Ken didn't respond to Garth. They waited for what seemed like an eternity, but it was probably five more minutes. "We're in position. Alex, you see us?" J.D. said.

"Got you. Garth, move to your right. More. More. Okay, don't go past where you are now to your left. Understand?"

"Don't go past here, or I'll get shot," Garth said. "Yeah, believe me, I understand."

"J.D., move to your left about a hundred feet." There was silence as his men moved into position. "Good. We're ready, Ken," Alex said.

"Hold on, I need to find a better angle over here," J.D. said quickly.

Dean pulled up behind them but stayed in his truck. They'd be moving soon. "Okay. Ready."

"Garth?" Ken asked.

"Ready," the man replied.

"We're en route."

Ken moved over, kissed her hard, and said, "Let's go."

Sam hopped out of his SUV and got into her cruiser. They pulled quietly down the road until they could be seen. Ken hit his lights and sirens, and so did she.

Men fell out of the buildings like ants. "Light them up, Alex," Ken commanded as they pulled into position.

Sam pulled her service pistol and was out of the car, crouched behind her car door, ready to fire, except the volley of rifle fire that landed between the men immediately stilled them.

"Hands up!" Ken's voice commanded over his vehicle's PA.

Two men started to move, but three quick whaps of a high-powered rifle stopped them. "On your knees. Now!" both she and Ken ordered. All the men, seven in total, dropped to their knees.

"Face down in the dirt," Ken ordered. Several of the men hesitated. Another whap of the rifle followed.

"Hands on the back of your head!" Sam yelled. That command everyone followed.

Over the radio, Ken moved Garth and J.D. "Move in, search the buildings, stay together," Ken ordered.

"Moving."

Sam pulled a handful of zip ties from her pouch, waiting for the all-clear. It took thirty minutes for all the buildings to be cleared. Finally, J.D. told them they could move.

"Search the truck," Ken reminded them. Sam covered the men as Garth and J.D. moved to the truck and searched the cab.

Garth pushed up the truck's back door as J.D. pointed his weapon in. "Damn. This is a Ferrari," J.D. said loud enough for everyone to hear.

"The back one is another one of those

McLaren's. There are two in the first barn," Garth added.

"How many vehicles?" Ken asked from where he stood.

J.D.'s head turned to look at him. "All totaled, maybe twenty and a handful of really nice bikes." Ken and Sam moved up. Ken kept his gun on the men, and Sam quickly started to cuff them. Garth and J.D. were there by the time they'd secured three men, and they helped with the other four.

"J.D., you and Garth gather the weapons and sit on these guys. Sam and I will do ID, rights advisement, and question them." He keyed his mic and said, "Alex and Brian, thanks for your help. I'll see you back in town."

"Roger. We're out," Alex's reply came back over the radio.

Sam did a pat down on the first man. She pulled out a wallet and tossed it to Ken. Together, they got the guy up and walked him back to Ken's SUV. They pulled the tailgate down and sat the man on the edge. He did the rights advisement, and Sam recorded it on her body cam.

"Now, Bradley, do you want a lawyer, or do you want a chance of going home sometime before your eightieth birthday?" Ken asked the man.

"Fuck you. I want a lawyer."

Ken sighed and moved the man where Garth could watch him, but the suspect couldn't talk to the other witnesses. Working as a team, they processed four more of the men, all of whom requested a lawyer before they hit pay dirt.

"Bob, you want a lawyer?" Ken asked after advising him of his rights.

"Man, I didn't do anything but drive the damn truck. I was too damn tired to drive back, so I crashed in the barn."

"Well, Bob, you see, we're in a bit of a predicament. You're here, and this, as you can see, is a high-end vehicle theft ring. A multi-million-dollar ring just by the vehicles here."

"But I didn't know that."

"Right. Of course, you didn't." Ken chuckled. "If you can't give us anything, you'll be processed just like the rest."

The man was silent for a moment. "I can tell you where the big shop is, where I picked up this load. I can also tell you who pays me."

Ken nodded. "So, you're waiving your rights to a lawyer, and you're going to help us?"

"Yeah, but you'll take that into account, right? I got a kid I need to support."

"Well, Bob, I'll make sure the DA knows you helped. She's a good person, and I know she'll take kindly to any information you can give us."

Sam wrote as Bob spoke. Then she cut his zip ties so he could sign his statement and re-cuffed him when he was done. After they'd finished with him, they brought the last man up.

"So, Thomas, I've read you your rights. I know where the vehicles are coming from and who's paying all of you. You're going to jail for a long time. Now, if there's something else you could tell me, I might be able to talk to the DA for you. You're wearing a wedding band. Do you want your wife to be without you for the next twenty or thirty years? Oh, just so you know, South Dakota jails don't have that overcrowding problem that the bigger states have. You'll do every day. Good time is discretionary up here."

"How do I know I'll be taken care of?" The man stared at Ken, then looked at Sam.

"Because, sir, you have my word. Up here, that means something. Men live and die by their word. I'll talk to the DA, and if you give me enough, she'll consider it." Ken adjusted his cowboy hat on his head and stared at the man.

"Bradley's in charge here. He's been here since

the start. We move approximately fifty cars a month. We can only work at night and not on the weekends now that hunting season has started. The sheriff, he's getting paid off. Bradley pays him cash every month. Meets him somewhere."

"How much?" Sam asked as she continued to write.

"Five thousand dollars a month," Thomas spat out.

"How do you know that?"

"Because I went with Bradley once, and the bastard counted it out on the hood of his police vehicle."

"What else can you tell us?"

"Names, people who run shit. Locations, routes, warehouses. I got it all. I listened just in case something like this happened. I ain't saying anything more until I get a guarantee in writing. I don't want to serve time."

"You just sit tight," Ken said. "I'll get you that meeting with the DA." When Sam returned from putting Thomas where J.D. and Garth could watch him, Ken told her, "I think it's time to call in the Bureau of Investigations."

"They'll need to process the scene," Sam agreed. She moved around the corner of the SUV and made sure no one could see her. "Holy shit, Ken! You just busted this ring open."

"We got lucky." Ken rubbed the back of his neck. "And we still have a lot of work to do, but..." He smiled at her. "I'm not the stupid rock Colby thought I was."

"What?" Sam gasped. "He called you stupid? Anyone who spent more than a minute with you knows that was an absolute lie."

Ken nodded. "Hold on." He picked up his radio. "Dot, this is Ken."

"Go ahead."

"We're clear here. The suspects have been processed. Call in the Bureau of Investigations. We'll keep the area secure until they arrive."

"They're already here. When you called them this morning, they must've headed out." Dot seemed to be chuckling. "I was eating lunch when they descended on the place."

"Well, send them out past the Hollisters' ranch about five miles. Have them look for Dean's game warden vehicle. He'll lead them back to us."

"I copy. Need anything else?" Dot asked.

"Yeah. Can you get me the number to the DA's office? I have some people who want to talk to her."

"I can do that, and you just made all these officers sitting in our lobby smile and do fist bumps." Dot laughed. The sound of celebrations behind her came over the radio, too.

"Glad they're happy," Ken said. "Call Eli from the power company to see if we can borrow his generator-powered light unit. I think we'll be working through the night."

"You got it," Dot said. "I'll call the diner and see if we can get meals for all of you set up, too."

"Thanks. We'll need that old van the church uses to transport these guys."

"I'll call Father Murphey. How many do you have?"

"Seven. Two are being transported separately, so the van will work."

"I copy all. I'll be here until you tell me to go home."

"Thanks, Dot. I'm clear." Ken put down the mic and looked at her. "Looks like you can put in your two weeks' notice."

Sam smiled and leaned forward. "Kiss me, sheriff; we probably won't get another chance for quite a while."

Ken leaned forward and grabbed her by the neck of her Kevlar. He tugged her in and kissed her until her brain melted. She was reluctant to open her eyes and break the spell when he released her. When she did, she saw his smiling face.

"You're going to marry me," he said as if he still didn't believe the words.

"I am. When the time is right."

"The time is right," he said, pulling her into him again.

"Hey, Ken? Oh, damn, I mean, dang. Sorry." J.D. turned around.

"What do you need?" Ken laughed as Sam stepped back to a respectable distance.

"One of the guys said he changed his mind and wants to talk to you."

Ken looked at her. "Ready to write some more?"

"As long as you readvise him of his rights and he waives counsel on the record." Sam wasn't going to let anyone walk on a technicality.

"Sounds like a plan. Bring him on back, J.D."

CHAPTER 17

Ken and the crew worked alongside the team that had responded from the South Dakota Bureau of Investigation. The highway patrol sent up a transport for the prisoners, so the church van wasn't needed. Sam visited with the troopers, who responded before they were put to work. Sure, they were being used as assistants, but they all kicked ass and worked through the night. By the time the sun had come up the next morning, Alex's tow truck and a semi with a vehicle hauler attached that the bureau had rented were lined up on the highway, waiting for the all-clear to come in and load the vehicles.

Ken was glad to see Brian and Phil were there

to help Alex and the semi driver as they worked out how to load the vehicles that didn't run. The bureau people had left, following the semi out of the homestead area.

"I'm hungry," J.D. said. "Too tired to eat, though."

"I'll buy lunch at the diner," Ken told everyone.

"Thanks, but I'm ready to drop," Garth said. "I'm heading home to a shower and sleep."

"Me, too." Dean yawned. "I'll see you around."

"Thanks for the help," Ken said again. Garth gave him a thumbs up. Dean lifted a hand as he walked toward his truck.

"I'll take a raincheck, Ken. The missus will need an update pretty darn soon, or I'll be sleeping in the doghouse."

"Let me know if you need backup." Ken chuckled.

"Don't think I won't!" J.D. hollered after the two men made their way to the game warden's vehicle. "Hey, Dean, wait for me. I need a lift to Trent's to pick up my vehicle."

Ken walked over to Sam. "Food, then bed."

"I'm starving," she admitted. They had sandwiches from the diner at about four yesterday

KEN

afternoon, and he was starving, too. Sam chuckled. "I'd even eat beets right now."

Ken laughed. "That's desperation."

"It is. I'll meet you at the diner." She went to move away, but he held her next to him. "I was serious when I said it was time."

Sam stared up at him. "I know. I'll marry you, but I want a full wedding. I want Carol as my maid of honor. My mom and dad have a savings account just for my wedding. But I don't want the stress of planning a wedding until after I take the bar."

Ken smiled down at her. "Then we have a timeline."

"We do." She toed up and kissed him.

They drove to the diner, and as they walked in, the entire place quieted.

"Did you get them?" Edna asked.

"All of them that were out there," Ken said. A round of applause sounded, and he blushed.

He almost reached the booth before Father Murphey asked, "Are you going to tell us about it?"

Ken looked back at the upturned faces. "It's an ongoing investigation." He glanced at Sam, who winked at him. "But there was over a couple million dollars worth of cars and motorcycles at the old homestead. The Bureau of Investigations

249

has taken custody of it, and what will come to be will be based on their continuing investigation into what several suspects told us."

"But you get the credit for the bust, right?" Carson Schmidt asked from the booth where he was sitting with Tegan Wells.

"Yeah. We all do. Sam, J.D., Garth, and Dean will all get credit for this, too." He'd love to give Alex and Nail credit, but he wouldn't mention them unless asked.

"Was Colby involved?" Edna wanted to know.

Ken made a show of thinking about how to answer the question before nodding. "Yeah, he was." He lifted his hand as the questions started to bombard him. "And I'm not saying another word about it. We've been up for way too long, and we're hungry."

"Two specials," Corrie said as she put down two platters of chicken fried steak, mashed potatoes, and roasted carrots. "I'll get you your soda, Ken, and an iced tea for you, Sam." Corrie turned and looked at the crowd. "Let them eat in peace."

Ken chuckled as he sat down. Corrie was right back with the drinks, and they dug in. "I needed this," Sam said. She pushed a stray lock of hair that had slipped from her bun behind her ears.

"You worked your ass off. I'm proud of all of you," Ken said before he took another bite.

Sam finished chewing before she spoke clearly and a bit too loudly, "It was a bust of a lifetime. You did that. You took the information, and you devised a plan." Sam's voice carried in the suddenly quiet diner. "You were the one that made it all happen, Ken. You're sharing the glory, but you would have taken the blame by yourself if it had gone bad. That's why you should be the next sheriff. You care for this county like no one ever has. Law enforcement runs through your veins. You're a natural protector and caretaker. You deserve to be elected sheriff when that twit Colby is sent to jail."

Allison turned around in her booth. "She's right, Ken. You've always taken care of the people in this county. You need to run."

Edna nodded. "Yes, yes, you do. I don't think anyone would run against you."

"Concur," Carson Schmidt said.

"I second that," Tegan Wells chimed in. There was a chorus of agreement, and Ken felt his face getting warm. Sam smiled at him and winked.

Ken turned around to address the crowd.

"Thank you. If there's a special election, I'll throw my hat in the ring."

"Hallelujah, and pass the salt, please," Father Murphey said, causing the diner to laugh.

After things settled a bit, Ken kicked Sam's foot under the table. She looked up at him. "What?"

"You did that on purpose."

She smiled. "Well, maybe."

"I owe you one," Ken said with a smile.

"Oh, I'll take you up on that as soon as we get home," Sam said before taking a drink of her iced tea.

"Yeah?" Ken leaned forward, keeping his voice low so no one would hear him. "Not too tired?"

"I think I can keep my eyes open for a bit longer," Sam said, wiping her mouth with her napkin. "Are you done?" She nodded to the remaining food on his plate.

"Yep. Couldn't eat another bite." Hell, he couldn't even remember what he'd been eating. He wiped his mouth and stood up, then took out his wallet.

"Those meals have already been paid for," Corrie said from behind him.

"By who?" Ken spun and asked.

"Can't remember," Corrie said as she hustled

past. "But they are. Get out of here so I can seat more people, would you?"

Ken opened his wallet and put down tip money. "Thank you to whoever did that. I can't accept things like that anymore. I don't want people to think I'm taking advantage of situations."

"We know you don't," Allison said from where she sat with Kathy Prentiss. "No one here would claim you do."

"Well, thank you," Ken said. Sam stood up, and they walked out of the diner and to their separate vehicles.

"See you at home," Ken said as he ducked into his SUV. He pulled out after Sam and followed her to his place. *Their* place.

He called Dot on the way home and told her to call him on his cell if he were needed and that he would crash for the day. She assured him that everything was quiet. He pulled in behind Sam's patrol car and headed inside. At the door was one of her boots. A few feet farther was the other one. Her gun belt was hooked to the coat rack. Ken pushed the front door closed and locked it behind him. He removed his gun belt and placed it on the last hook available. Sam's shirt was in the hall, along with her Kevlar vest. Her pants were outside the bedroom door. Ken opened the half-closed door and found her panties and bra. At the bathroom door were her socks. He pushed the door open and found her standing beside the shower. "How did you find me, sheriff?"

"I followed the clues," Ken said as he pulled off his shirt and ripped the Velcro straps holding his Kevlar in position. He shed the vest and pulled off his t-shirt.

Sam turned on the water before she moved to help him take off his belt. She dropped to her knees and pulled off his cowboy boots and socks. Reaching up, she unfastened his uniform slacks and pulled them down to his knees. Before he could take them off, her hand circled his cock, and her mouth found the tip. On reflex, he jolted forward, and his cock lodged toward the back of her throat. He tried to back off, but she grabbed his ass and pushed him forward again. His eyes slammed shut as her hot, wet mouth worked on his shaft. Her tongue circled the cap, and she moved forward again. His hands found her hair, which was still in that damn bun. He slid his hand to the back of her neck, not to push her, but to ground himself. She cupped his balls and squeezed just the slightest amount.

"Oh, damn. Babe, you have to stop, or I'll come."

She squeezed his balls again and pushed his cockhead to the back of her throat. Seeing stars used to be just a saying, but holy hell, white exploding bursts fired behind his closed eyes. He dropped his head back and let himself go. The sensations of her mouth and hands were too much.

He looked down at her. "I'm going to come."

Her eyes opened, and she stared up at him. He would always remember the look he saw there. Seconds later, his eyes slammed shut as his body let go. He expected her to stop, to catch his release in her hand. She didn't. She sucked as he shot again. His arm shot out to the wall. She swirled her tongue around his cock. He shivered at the intensity of the sensation around his now over-sensitive shaft. Lifting her chin, he slipped out of her mouth. He helped her up and kissed her. His taste on her tongue was as intimate as he'd ever been with a woman.

When he broke the kiss, he held her against himself. "You should have let me finish inside you."

"Next time. Now, we take a long hot shower, and then, we sleep." Pulling away, she slid her hand down his arm to grab his hand.

"That's not fair to you." Ken frowned as they made their way into the shower.

She turned to him and put her arms around his neck. "I got to watch you last night. Every time I looked up from what I was doing, I watched you in your element. The people from the bureau respected your opinion and input. They asked for your suggestions, and you earned their respect. I saw all of that. I wanted to claim what was mine. I wanted to make sure you knew who you belonged to. Who would be waiting for you when you came home. Who would be here for you when you had a bad day and to celebrate when you had a great one. I know we're going to make it, Ken. I know it because I'm in love with you and committed to loving you for the rest of my life."

Ken stared down at her. "I'm the luckiest man alive. Everything is better with you with me. You were sent from heaven to answer a prayer I've said for years. You're the only one who can be my friend, my lover, and someday, the mother of my children."

"I am that person." She lifted and kissed him on the chin. "And you're mine."

He wrapped his arms around her and let the connection of their souls entwine around his heart in an intricate series of links built on friendship and forged by the heat of love. A smile formed on his face that nothing could wipe off. Two weeks from then, she'd be there full-time. They would get married. Life couldn't get any better.

CHAPTER 18

Sam picked up her cell call on the hands-free device and answered Ken. "Hey, I'm on my way back north." She'd been called to the office to do some paperwork for her forwarding address so her last check could be sent to her. Five more days, and she would be a full-time resident of Bridger County.

"Good. I just wanted to let you know I need to head out to the Marshall Ranch. I have to return some equipment I borrowed. I wasn't sure when you were going to get home. I didn't want you to worry."

"Thank you. I'm about an hour away from home. I can't believe all this will be done in five days."

"Yep, and then you crack open that study material your parents bought you, and it's nose to the grindstone." Ken chuckled.

"Gladly. You scheduled for vacation the week of the bar, right?"

"I did. I'll take you to the exam and be there when you come out brain-dead." He laughed again.

"You have no idea how right you are. I was talking to a couple of old classmates this morning about what to expect, and to a person, they said it was the most taxing test they've ever taken."

"I don't doubt it," Ken said. "I'm almost to the Marshalls'. Be safe. I love you."

"I love you, too, and I'm *always* safe." She chuckled as he made a noise. "But yes, I'll be extra careful."

"Thank you. Bye."

"Bye." She disconnected and continued her cruise on Highway 85 North. About twenty miles up the road, she saw a car ahead of her. It swerved over the yellow line, then overcorrected, and almost went off the road into the ditch. She sped up and watched it swerve into the oncoming traffic lane before jerking back to its lane.

She picked up the mic. "Dispatch, this is K29." She clicked on her blue lights and hit the siren.

"K29, go ahead," the dispatcher responded.

"Affirm. Initiating a traffic stop on a late-model sedan. Erratic driving, crossing the middle line, failure to control the vehicle." As she got closer, she determined the make, model, and license plate and called it in. The driver pulled over, and she stopped behind it, turning on her dash cam to record the stop. She made sure her body cam was turned on, too. Getting out of the car, Sam carefully approached the vehicle and ensured she was behind the driver's left shoulder when she stopped. Her hand was on her weapon. The safety strap was unfastened so she could draw the weapon if needed. The driver looked back at her.

"What's the problem, officer?" His voice was slurred, and his pupils were blown.

"Sir, I need you to turn off the vehicle and step out of the car."

"Why?" The man's demeanor changed in an instant. The smile dropped from his face, and his voice changed into a challenge.

"You were swerving and crossing the center line. Turn off the vehicle and get out, please."

"Sure." The driver turned forward. She watched carefully, but the man twisted quickly. She saw the weapon and moved, pulling her automatic out of its holster. Sam felt the blunt kick of the bullet before she heard the shot. Her head hit the pavement, and pain consumed her. She rolled and grabbed the mic clipped to her shoulder. "Trooper down. Trooper down. I've been shot."

She heard the dispatcher but was determined to pull herself out of the middle of the road. She crawled elbow over elbow, pulling her useless legs after her to the side of the road in front of her vehicle. She grabbed the mic. "Shot, lower gut. Need help." Sam started to shake. She couldn't die like that. She couldn't ...

* * *

"I APPRECIATE THE LOAN, sir. We didn't use them, then with the hustle and bustle, I neglected to bring them back."

"No worries, if I needed them, I'd have called." Frank dropped the NVGs on the swing beside him. "Did you hear that Colby is facing federal charges now?"

"No, sir, I didn't. How did that happen?" Ken leaned against the post of the porch to visit.

"Can't say as I know exactly. Something about the Bureau of Investigations being able to determine interstate dissemination of that stuff he had on the computer."

"Huh." Ken looked down at the toe of his cowboy boot. "And here I thought it was because he threatened the wrong person."

Frank Marshall grunted a laugh and pulled two pieces of taffy out of his pocket. "Well, you know what they say, son. Never bring a knife to a gunfight."

"Colby had no idea how big of a gunfight he was entering, did he?"

"He's never been out here. I haven't shared a damn thing with him. He always gave me pause. Never trusted him," Frank said as he unwrapped his taffy.

"I wish I hadn't," Ken said. His radio and cell phone went off at the same time.

"Looks like you're about to get busy," Frank said as he grabbed his radio from his belt.

"Go ahead, Dot."

"Ken, It's Sam. She's been shot. SDHP wants us to respond. We're closer!" Dot yelled over the radio.

As Ken bolted to his SUV, a sharp whistle stopped him. "Helicopter!" Frank pointed to the other side of the ranch with his phone plastered to his ear. Ken got into his SUV and tore over the hill. As he pulled up, he saw three people running to his location.

"Get in the back!" Dixon, or was it Drake, yelled. Ken didn't care. He opened the door and piled in. "Put on a headset! Where are we going?"

"She was about an hour south of here on Highway 85."

Doctor Adam Cassidy threw his bag into the helicopter. "I got the Mercy alert. What do we have?"

"Sam's been shot. The last time I talked to her, she was about an hour south of here. I don't have any further information." Ken grabbed what looked like an "oh shit" bar and held on as the helicopter lifted from the ground. The thing tipped forward as it moved until the rotors were up to speed, but damned if they weren't flying.

Ken strained to see the road. "We're going across Marshall land. That will cut time," either Dixon or Drake said to him. Ken nodded. He got it. He glanced at his watch and then back through the front of the helicopter. Damn it, the thing needed to fly faster.

Doc grabbed his arm. "I said, does she wear Kevlar?"

"Yes. Every day," Ken confirmed.

"Then we're looking at an extremity or lower abdomen injury." He shook Ken's arm again. "We'll do everything we can."

Ken nodded again. It seemed like forever before he saw the road. The helicopter veered to the left and flew over the highway heading south. "There." Dixon pointed to something on the horizon. Blue lights strobed beside the road.

Ken grabbed onto that bar again as they came in for a landing at full fucking speed, then swung around so he could see the car. Doc was out of the helicopter before it touched land. Ken was right behind him.

They skidded to a stop in front of the car. "Oh, fuck, babe." Ken knelt beside her and picked up her hand, taking her weapon from her.

"Get this shirt and Kevlar off her. I need to see what I'm working with." Doc unfastened her gun belt and ripped her pants, revealing her lower stomach. Ken ripped the buttons off her shirt and unfastened the Velcro. He slipped the front vest up over her head.

"Call this into your dispatch. Gunshot wound to the lower abdomen. No exit wound. She's unconscious and bleeding internally. We're taking her to Spearfish. Belle doesn't have the capabilities she's going to need. Once we're in the air, I'll have Dixon call it in, and they'll have a surgical team meet us."

Ken followed Doc's instructions, then ran to the helicopter, which had landed in the middle of the road. Dixon was running toward him with a stretcher. Ken raced back, and they carefully but quickly put her on the stretcher. Doc and Dixon lifted her, and Ken grabbed her weapon and gun belt. They had her in the back of the helicopter and were flying south in under five minutes from the time they landed.

Ken held her hand. "Hang on. You can't leave me yet."

"She's not going anywhere if I can help it," Doc said as he continued to work on her.

Ken prayed he was right. He stared down at the woman he loved. Her face was pale, making the light spray of freckles on her nose stand out. He touched her face and closed his eyes. *This can't be happening.*

It could have been twenty minutes or twenty days later when the helicopter landed; time had stopped for him. Sam's color had paled even more. Her lips were no longer pink but tinged with blue.

As soon as the door opened, Doc Cassidy was out of the compartment, and Ken grabbed the head of the stretcher. They unloaded her onto a gurney from the hospital, and Ken raced after the medical team as they traversed the parking lot and entered the hospital. Doc Cassidy spouted off her vitals and the information he knew. Ken was right beside them as they wheeled her into a room. Doc Cassidy grabbed him by the shoulder. "You can't go in there."

Ken blinked as the door shut in front of him. "Is she going to make it?"

"She made it this far. That means she's a fighter. But you might want to contact her supervisor and maybe her family."

Ken nodded and looked down at the gun belt in his hand. He lifted it. "The bullet." He put his thumbnail in the furrow the bullet had made in the leather.

Doc nodded. "I've got to get back to the helicopter. Is there anything I can do for you?"

"No." Ken shook his head. "Thank you. I couldn't have gotten her to help without you."

"We take care of our own, Ken. Call Frank and let him know how she's doing."

"As soon as I get an update. Thanks, Adam."

"I'd say anytime, but I think we need to limit this type of situation." Doc put a hand on his shoulder. "Take care."

Ken nodded and called Dot. He gave what information he had to her and asked her to contact Sam's department. He also told her that Doc Cassidy suggested her parents be called and asked her to do that.

"Oh, Ken." Dot's voice cracked.

"She's a fighter," he repeated. "She made it this far. She's a fighter."

"She is. I'll make those calls, and then, I'll start the prayer circle. For her and you."

"Thanks, Dot." Ken hung up and found a seat in the corner of the waiting room. He placed her gun belt over his thighs and stared down at the scar the bullet had made. Their profession was dangerous. He knew that. Her gun hadn't been fired. Whoever shot her did so without any warning.

"Ah, officer?" A nurse was in front of him. Ken stood up so fast he nearly knocked her onto her ass.

"I'm sorry." He grabbed her arm and steadied her.

"It's okay. They're taking your co-worker up to surgery. I'll show you the way. There's a waiting room that's a little more private." She motioned to the people in the emergency room.

Ken nodded. "Thank you."

He followed her through the series of turns and found himself in a small alcove with chairs identical to the one he'd been sitting in. His phone vibrated, and he frowned at the unknown number.

He was tempted not to answer but finally connected. "Zorn."

"Ken, this is Megan, Samantha's mother. Her father and I are on the way to a private airstrip near Pierre to catch a plane to Rapid."

"Ma'am, see if they can bring you to Spearfish. That's where we're at. The surgical center."

"You're on speaker phone, son," a man's voice said. "I'll do that. What the fuck happened?"

"She was on the way back up. She was an hour out. I don't know the particulars, but she must have made a traffic stop or stopped to help someone. She was shot in the lower abdomen. Entry but no exit wound, according to the doctor I had with me. We flew her via helicopter to Spearfish. She's strong, and she's a fighter." Ken fell back on what Adam had told him. It was his mantra, and he wouldn't let go of it.

"What about body cam or vehicle cam?"

KEN

"Sir, I stripped her out of her equipment at the scene. I didn't check. Getting her to a hospital was the priority. I have her service weapon with me."

"We'll be there as soon as possible. Someone from the troop should be there shortly."

"Yes, sir."

"I'll call as soon as we land," her mom said.

"Yes, ma'am," Ken said and hung up. He settled back into his chair and found a place on the wall to stare at. No news at that point was good news. He listened to the background noise of the hospital. A couple arrived and waited with him for about an hour. A doctor strode down the hall, and all three of them stood up. "Mr. and Mrs. DeAngelo?"

"Yes?" the woman said.

"Barrett is doing fine. His appendix was inflamed, and we got it before it burst. He's in recovery now, and a nurse will take you back soon."

Ken sat down again. The sound of boots walking on the tile again made him look up. A trooper strode down the hallway, stopping in front of Ken. "Sheriff Zorn?"

"Yeah." Ken stood.

"Have you had any updates?" the trooper asked

as he sat down beside him. "Sergeant Stapleton regrets he couldn't be here."

Ken huffed a bitter laugh at that. "No doubt." He glanced at the man next to him. "He doesn't like Sam."

"He doesn't like anyone," the trooper said. "My name's Tony. How's she doing?"

"In surgery. The doctor we flew down here with said she was strong enough to make it this far. Her dad asked about body cam and vehicle cam footage."

"Her dad? Why would he ask that?" Tony's brow furrowed. Ken glanced over at the man. He didn't seem like he was poking fun. "Reid Quinn, Superintendent of the South Dakota Highway Patrol, is her father."

"Holy shitballs." The man's jaw went slack. "I had no idea."

"Yeah, so getting that information for him would be important." Ken didn't know how Stapleton could justify staying away when one of his troopers had been shot, but that wasn't his problem to worry about.

"Yeah. We have two troopers on the way up. After processing her vehicle, they'll collect anything left from the scene."

Ken nodded. It was a crime. He knew that. He only hoped the fucker who shot her would be locked away until he rotted.

"Is that her service weapon?" Tony nodded to the gun belt.

"Yeah." Ken didn't offer to give it to him. It was his link to her, and he'd be damned if anyone was taking it right now.

"Wait, you said flew … How?"

"A rancher up north has a helicopter. I was at his place when the call came in. He offered it."

"Damn," Tony said again and hung his head. He glanced around the now-empty waiting room. "How long has she been in surgery?"

"Over three hours."

Tony sat with him for some time before he went and got each of them a pop. Ken took a hit of the sugar and realized how much he needed it. He glanced at the clock. Five hours. A hurried pair of steps down the hall made both him and Tony look up.

"Ken? You're Ken, right?" Megan Quinn ran up to him. When he nodded, she asked, "Have you heard anything?"

"No, ma'am. Not a word, but I'm not family. Maybe you could check in at the nurses' station?"

"That's a load of bullshit." Megan turned around. "You're engaged to my daughter. That makes you family. Reid, I'll be right back."

Reid Quinn was a tall and fit man, dressed in his trooper's uniform. The number of stars on the man's shoulders would dazzle anyone. "Trooper," Reid said. "Where's Stapleton?"

"Ah, sir, he sent his regrets. He was unable to make it. I'm Trooper Daniels, Tony Daniels."

Quinn shook the man's hand. "I need you to call your sergeant and tell him I'm here and want him here ASAP."

"Yes, sir. Excuse me, please." Tony strode down the hall and pulled out his cell phone.

"You're Ken Zorn?" Reid stared at him.

"I am." Ken stared right back.

"It's good to meet you finally. Sam has told us, and by us, I mean her mom, so much about you. She's in love with you."

"As I am with her, sir."

"My name is Reid. Sir is for the troopers and only because of these stars on my shoulders."

Ken tried to smile. "All right. Thank you."

"They said there hasn't been an update. The nurse will go ask if she can get any information."

Megan sat down beside Ken. "Tell me from the start what happened? Please?"

Ken drew a deep breath and told them what had happened and the fact that Frank had stopped and offered the use of his helicopter. "I don't know more than that. Tony said they'd dispatched someone up north to recover her vehicle and anything left on the scene."

"Well, at least that's something," Reid said, wiping his face with his hand. They sat silently for another hour before a quick striding doctor headed their way. Ken saw him first and stood up. Sam's mother and father were on their feet seconds later.

"I'm looking for Mr. and Mrs. Quinn?"

"That's us. This is Sam's fiancé." Megan grabbed Ken's arm.

"Good. I'm Dr. Justice. Samantha is one tough lady. We've repaired the damage to her intestines, but unfortunately, we couldn't save her uterus. We made sure we didn't miss any small nicks to her intestines, which is what took us so long."

"But she's going to be okay, right?" Ken stepped forward. He needed to hear the confirmation.

The doctor nodded. "She's in recovery now. I'm

guardedly optimistic at this time. She'll be monitored closely. We're confident we were able to close all the bleeders. However, infection is our primary concern with any gastrointestinal compromise. That bullet could have caused unrecoverable damage had it gone anywhere but where it did. She's a lucky woman."

"Can we see her?" Megan asked.

"A nurse will come to you when she's out of recovery."

"Thank you, doctor." Reid offered his hand.

The doctor shook it. "She's a fighter."

Ken dropped down into his chair and covered his face. The emotion he'd been holding at bay filled him, and he didn't give a fuck who saw the tears. She'd made it through the surgery. Thank God.

He felt Megan next to him and Reid's hand on his shoulder. "I'm sorry," he apologized and wiped at the tears.

"Don't be." Megan put her head on his shoulder. "You love her. Never apologize for tears shed for those you love."

"Amen." Reid wiped at his own tears.

"Superintendent Quinn," a voice said from the hallway.

Ken looked up. "Ah, Stapleton, what was so

important you couldn't be here to support your trooper?" Reid's voice was icy and cold.

Stapleton crossed his arms over his chest. "I sent a representative. I was handling notifications."

Quinn frowned. "Funny, I didn't receive any notifications from your department. Her fiancé's office called me, but you didn't."

"I'm sure your office was notified in due course." Stapleton rocked back on his heels. "Is there anything else?"

Reid stepped over to the man. Ken couldn't make out what was said, but Stapleton's face turned red. Reid pointed down the hall and said something else. Stapleton turned on his heel and marched out of sight.

"Thank God she won't work for that bastard any longer," Reid said when he turned back to them.

Ken nodded. "Sam's told me the digs he gets at her. He hates that she's your daughter."

"Oh, no doubt." Megan patted his thigh. "Victor Stapleton asked me out the night I met Reid. I turned him down that night and every other time he asked for the next six months."

"Yeah, I wasn't the fastest on the uptake." Reid chuckled and rubbed the back of his neck.

"Anyway, when Reid finally asked me out, I said yes. Victor saw us. He's hated Reid ever since. Plus, Reid was promoted over him. A perfect storm to cause a spiteful man." Megan sighed. "But this was low."

"I'll handle that when I get back to the office. After we make sure Sam's on the mend," Reid said.

"Mr. and Mrs. Quinn? I can take one of you back now."

"You go," Reid told Megan.

She glanced at Ken, who said, "Yes, go. I'll wait." He didn't want to. He wanted to rush in there and make sure she was breathing, to feel her warm skin, to see the color of her lips, to prove to himself she was still with him.

Megan stood up and followed the nurse as Reid sat down next to him. "She'll be okay."

"She's a fighter," Ken said. He glanced over at his future father-in-law. "Thank you for making her have a backup plan."

Reid nodded. "Did she ever tell you I had a dream about her being shot?"

Ken blinked and shook his head. "No, sir."

"Yeah, I did. Before she joined, it was so damn real. I hardly slept for a week, and I've never forgotten it. That girl." He chuckled. "She's her mom's and my world. I can only imagine how this has affected you."

"I don't think it's fully hit me," Ken said, looking at the clock. "I should call up north and tell people she made it through surgery."

"You do that, son. She loves that little town up there."

"And they love her, sir." Ken took out his phone and dialed Frank Marshall's number first.

"How is she?" Frank didn't even say hello.

"She made it through surgery. Her mom is with her now. Thank you again, sir, for the use of the helicopter and the guys helping me out."

"After everything you've done for us, no thanks are necessary. Take care of that woman, Ken."

"Yes, sir, I will." He hung up and called Dot. The woman started to cry when he told her she was out of surgery. "Dot, after you blow your nose, let everyone know, okay?"

"I will."

"Oh, and tell them not to come down yet. I don't know when she can have visitors."

"Will do. But you'll let us know, right?"

"I will," Ken assured her. He hung up the phone and realized he still held her gun belt. "I should have let Tony take this with him when he left. I just couldn't let it go."

"I'll make a call and get a trooper back here to take it and secure it," Reid said as he exhaled. "Do you have a hotel room up here?"

Ken blinked. He hadn't thought about anything other than finding out how Sam was doing. "No, sir."

"I'll call around and get that settled, too. I doubt they'll let either of us see her tonight. I've held vigils in too many of these rooms to recall. Tomorrow, we'll see our girl."

"No, sir, I'm not leaving. You two go ahead and get some sleep. I would just go crazy being away from her." He'd plant his ass in one of those chairs and stare at the damn door all night if he had to, but he wasn't leaving.

About ten minutes later, Megan came out of the same door that she went into. "She opened her eyes for a minute but went back to sleep. The nurse in the recovery room said all her vitals are just where they want them to be." Tears welled up in her eyes. "She's not out of the woods, but she's strong."

Ken watched as Reid hugged Megan, only turning at the sound of approaching footsteps.

KEN

Tony was back in civilian clothes. "Hey, any news?" He shook Ken's hand.

"She's out of surgery," Ken told him.

"Good. Prognosis?"

"Guardedly optimistic," Reid answered.

"I'm glad. I thought perhaps I might be of some help. I have an SUV outside. Does anyone need a ride?"

Reid nodded. "We do. While her mom was in with her, I got us a hotel room. We'll get some rest and be back bright and early tomorrow morning."

Tony turned to Ken, who lifted Sam's gun belt and asked. "Can you secure this? I'm staying."

Tony took the belt with her service weapon in it. "You got it."

Turning to Reid, Ken said, "I'll call you, sir, if there's any change in her condition."

"I've told them you're family, so there shouldn't be any problems." Megan sighed. "I don't want to leave."

Reid put his arm around her. "I know, but being exhausted tomorrow won't help her."

Megan nodded. They said their goodbyes, and Ken walked to the window at the end of the hall. He didn't know how long he stared at the pine trees. Some time later, an older nurse walked down to him. "Hi, officer, I'm Tally, the night shift supervisor. Can I help you?"

Ken tried to smile at her. He wasn't sure if he pulled it off. "My fiancée, Samantha Quinn, was shot today while on patrol. She's in recovery."

Tally frowned. "No, sir, she's in a room now. Didn't anyone tell you?" Ken shook his head. Tally made a sound of annoyance in her throat. "We aren't supposed to let visitors stay. I'm surprised no one asked you to leave."

"I'm not going anywhere. I can't ... She's my world." He rubbed his face.

Tally pulled her bottom lip between her teeth and narrowed her eyes. "The policy states *visitors* can't stay past visiting hours. The *only* exceptions are clergy and police officers. And you, sir, are the exception." She lowered her eyes to his name tag. "Officer Zorn, would you like to accompany me to her room?"

"It's sheriff, ma'am, and please, call me Ken." He extended his hand.

"Ken, it is." She shook his hand. "There will be a bunch of machines that will monitor her vitals, and she's got an IV for antibiotics. Abdominal injuries are notorious for infections. She's been given a sedative, so she'll probably sleep through the night." He followed Tally through the halls and around several corners. Finally, right across from another nurses' station, she pointed to a door. "Here we are." Tally moved out of his way, and he walked into the small room.

Slowly, he went up to the foot of the bed and stared at the woman he loved. She was pale, but nothing like the blue-tinged color she'd been earlier in the day. Her hair was still in a braid and over her shoulder. He scanned the machines and moved to the hand that didn't have an IV running to the back of it. An oxygen monitor was on her finger, but he cupped her hand, careful not to dislodge the clip.

"Here." Tally was at the door. "Sorry, this is the best I can do." She carried in a small plastic chair.

Ken thanked her and sat down beside Samantha's bed. He put his cowboy hat on her small bedside table and sat down, still holding her hand. His thumb rubbed back and forth over the top of her hand. "You scared me half to death," Ken whispered. "I don't think I've ever prayed so hard in my life." He looked up at her. "They fixed you up. Patched all the holes." He lowered his eyes to her stomach. "They said they had to remove your uterus. I don't know how you'll take to that news, but, babe, I'm not worried. If we want, we can adopt, but that's years down the road." He sighed and dropped his forehead to her hand. "I'll do whatever it takes to make you happy. You just need to get better." Closing his eyes, he said another prayer.

CHAPTER 19

Sam woke in layers. Her senses peeled back to consciousness bit by bit. She remembered waking momentarily and then dropping back to sleep numerous times. Confusion and fear hit hard when she could finally open her eyes. The lights in the hallway illuminated the hospital room. She blinked and turned her head. Ken. He was sitting in a chair, but her hospital bed supported his arms and head as he slept. She lifted her hand and placed it on his head. A feeling of numbness holding back ... something ... was displaced momentarily when her hand landed in his hair. He moved and sighed. She closed her eyes but opened them when she remembered—She'd been shot. She moved her toes. Thank God. She couldn't feel them when she was crawling to the side of the road. She moved her fingers in Ken's hair. She was alive. Thank God.

As a nurse walked into her room. she turned her head to look at the woman.

"How are you feeling?" the nurse whispered.

Sam tried to talk, but she was so dry she had to peel her tongue from the roof of her mouth. "Like I've been shot."

The nurse chuckled, and Ken's head popped off the bed. He was on his feet a second later. "Babe." Ken hovered over her. "I love you."

Sam smiled. "Love you." That was all she managed. She hated the cotton feeling in her mouth. Her eyelids were so damn heavy.

"Your fiancée has a sense of humor, Ken. I came in to let you know shift change was about to happen. I've talked to the daytime nurse, and she's cool with you being here. We have policy to cover us."

"Thank you, Tally."

Ken's hand cupped her cheek, and she opened her eyes that she didn't know she'd shut. "You're going to be okay, babe."

"Shooter?" She closed her eyes again and sighed.

"I don't know." Ken's voice was such a wonderful sound. "Sleep, sweetheart. I'll be here when you wake up. You're going to be okay."

Sam sighed again and closed her eyes. She knew he would be here, protecting and watching over her. He was her guardian, and she was safe.

* * *

"Mom, could you help with my socks?" Sam looked at her feet. She'd managed to get the joggers with a drawstring on, but damn it, she wasn't bending over anymore if she could help it.

Her mom stopped packing her hospital things and came over. "I told you to let me help you with your pants." Her mom lifted her eyebrows as she bent to put on Sam's socks.

"The doctor said I could bend if I could tolerate it and to go slowly. It took five minutes to get these on. I have to get stronger, and I can't do that if I let everyone do everything for me." She was so over being in the hospital.

"You can't get stronger if you rip your stitches and end up back in that bed," her mom retorted.

Sam glanced at the bed she was sitting on. "Well, that's true."

Her mom's eyebrows popped up to her hairline. "Did you just admit I was right?"

Sam chuckled and then held her stomach. "Don't make me laugh. When are Ken and Dad supposed to be here?"

Her mom looked at the clock. "Anytime now. Dad called when they started back from Hollister. He said the people at the diner were pretty intense with their questioning."

Sam smiled as her mom picked up the slip-on tennis shoes she bought in Spearfish. For that matter, all the clothes she was wearing were purchased by her mom, so Ken didn't have to go back to Hollister without her. He was getting her SUV to drive them back. Her dad took him up in the rental they'd gotten. "Those people are the best," Sam said, holding her mom's hand to stand up. "Damn, I feel as weak as a kitten."

"That's to be expected. Are you sure you don't want me to stay with you for a week or two?" Her mom helped her to the chair in her room.

Sam sat down and sighed. "God, it's so good to sit down." She was so over lying still.

"Here we go," Janice, one of the daytime nurses, said as she walked in with a folder. "We have the discharge paperwork." Janice reviewed the doctor's instructions, wound care, and what to watch out for. Sam made sure she understood everything, including the physical limitations. She didn't want to hinder her rehab by being stupid. Janice opened one of the bottles and shook out a tablet. "This is your pain med. You're going to thank me for this. The drive home will not be comfortable without it."

She took the pill and water from Janice. The woman had never steered her wrong before, and she wouldn't begin questioning the nurse's directions as she left. Her mom took the folder and the medications. "Ken will have to get these refilled." Her mom looked at the bottles. "They gave you a week's supply. Are you sure you don't want me to come stay with you?"

"I'll be just fine. I'll sit in the rocking chair on the porch and study. Ken won't let me lift a finger, and I'm not going to do anything stupid." She smiled. "Thank you for taking such good care of Ken and me."

Her mom sat down on the hospital bed and sighed. "He's an amazing man. You were right about him."

"Yeah, I was." She smiled to herself. He'd been so worried about her. She'd been upset when she found out she'd had what amounted to a hysterectomy. She wanted to have kids someday. It was a vague thing, but it was still a loss. Ken sat with her the entire afternoon, and they talked about their future and what that looked like now. She cried, and he held her. He'd called Dr. Wheeler and admitted doing so before having the conversation. The doctor said the grief would come and go and that he would talk with her whenever she needed help. But what she remembered most was that Ken told her they could adopt or foster if she wanted children. He would do whatever she needed. Of course, he would. She smiled at the memory. They'd had long conversations while she was in the hospital. Garth, J.D., and Douglas were handling the county along with an assist from a deputy loaned to them by Harding County to the north. The person who had shot her was a known drug user in North Dakota. He was stopped when his vehicle description hit the airwaves. Hank Bartel tried to shoot another law enforcement officer and paid with his life. Ken had held her hand when Tony came by to brief her on that takedown. She grieved for Bartel's family and the loss of life, but thankfully, he would never harm another person.

Through it all, her rock was Ken. He watched over her mom and dad, ensuring they were cared for and had everything they needed. Her love for him was stronger than any emotion she'd ever experienced. The man was perfect for her.

"When did you say we'll start planning the wedding?" Her mom's question popped her out of her musing.

Sam held her abs and chuckled. "Will you stop asking that?"

"No," her mom sassed back.

"After I pass the bar." It seemed like Sam had that conversation with her mom about every three hours.

"Then you better pass it the first time. You know I'll work it behind the scenes, right?"

"As long as you don't pick out my dress or the reception food." Sam pointed at her mom. "I will not wear a mermaid dress, and there will be no beets at my wedding."

Her mom laughed. "I think you'd look amazing in that type of dress, but maybe we can go to Denver or Minneapolis for a long weekend and try on dresses. Wouldn't that be fun?"

"It would be, but I was thinking of something different."

"You are not wearing jeans to get married." Her mom's statement was immediate.

Sam laughed and winced as she covered her incision site with her hand. "Stop, Mom. No, Kayla Bryce has a tailor shop in Hollister. She makes wedding gowns by hand. I've seen pictures of what she's capable of doing. Maybe I could use yours and have her modify it to fit me."

Her mom lifted her hand to her mouth. "You'd want to do that?"

"If it's okay with you?"

Her mom started fanning her face. "Oh, God, yes! Now, you're going to make me cry."

"What?" Her dad walked in right before Ken. "Why are you crying?"

"Because I'm happy." Her mom sniffed and continued to fan at her eyes so her makeup wouldn't run.

Ken walked over and dropped down to kiss Sam. "Are you ready to get out of here?"

"A thousand times, yes." She smiled at him.

"I'll go ask Janice for a wheelchair." Her dad was out of the door a second later.

"Thank you for letting me borrow your husband," Ken told her mom. "We popped into the diner for lunch. Everyone says hi, by the way. Edna and Corrie have organized a meal train for us, and some women have scheduled cleaning and laundry days. Although I'm quite capable of cleaning and doing laundry." Ken rubbed the back of his neck. "But judging by the mood in that café, if I objected, I think they might have lynched me."

"That sounds perfect." Her mom put the last of her items into the plastic bag she'd been filling.

"What?" both Ken and Sam asked at the same time.

"What?" Her mom looked up at them. "Oh, not the lynching! The food and cleaning."

Ken laughed. "Thank goodness."

"Here we are." Her dad pushed the wheelchair into the room. "I can't push you out. Hospital policy."

Janice laughed. "I wouldn't get to say goodbye to our favorite patient and her family."

Ken helped her into the chair as Janice waived off the orderly, who offered to take them to the front of the facility. "Remember, we want an invite to the wedding." She hugged Samantha. "Listen to your body and take care of yourself."

"Thank you." Sam hugged the woman back. She'd been so kind and helpful.

"All right, dear. Hug your baby. We need to

head home." Her dad bent down and kissed her on the forehead. "Love you, ladybug."

Sam smiled up at her dad. "Love you, too."

"I'm calling every day." Her mom bent down and kissed her on the cheek.

"I'll answer every day. Love you, Momma."

"Love you, too." Her mom went over to Ken and hugged him. "If you need me to come and whip her into shape, just call."

"I will." Ken shook her dad's hand. "Drive carefully, sir."

"You, too." Her dad pulled Ken into one of those man-clench things, and they pounded on each other's back.

Ken turned to her and took the plastic bag from her lap, placing it in the back seat of the SUV. He helped her into the front seat and carefully crossed the seat belt low over her lap. *Finally*, she was on her way home.

CHAPTER 20

Samantha arched her back. The bar exam consisted of four sections. Essay, performance test, and multi-state bar exam. It also included one Indian law question. Samantha had studied for months for the Indian law question and still wasn't sure if she got the answer right. But it was all she could do. If she didn't pass, she'd take it again in July.

She watched out the window and waited for Ken to pull up. She'd texted him when she'd finished. He was driving over from the hotel, which was nearby. When she saw their newly bought used SUV pull up, she pushed open the door to the parking lot and was blasted with cold air. February in South Dakota was bitter cold.

She trotted out to the vehicle and got in. "Well, how do you think it went?" Ken asked as he leaned over and kissed her.

"I really have no idea. I think I did well in the essay and multi-state portions, but the other two ... Man, I have no clue." She dropped her head back on the headrest. "How did it go with you?"

"I met with the DA to go over my testimony. Dot did hers by video, which the DA was good with. No need to make her drive down in this weather."

"So, no more delays? Colby's finally going to court?" The man's lawyer was inventive in how he'd delayed the trial. Of course, Colby getting jumped by some inmates who didn't like what he was in jail for and ending up in the hospital added a couple of months to the delay and an emergency request to change the venue. The judge agreed and moved the trial to Lawrence County, specifically Rapid City.

"Do you know when you'll have to be back down?"

"The court date is in May. By then, we'll have the paperwork approved to hire a new deputy in a temporary capacity." Without Colby robbing the county every month, they could afford another full-time deputy along with their part-timers, Garth and Douglas.

Ken pulled back onto the road and headed in the opposite direction of the hotel. "Where are we going?"

"I have something I need to do." Ken turned on his blinker and pulled onto the main drag.

"It won't take long, will it? I need some aspirin and maybe a drink. I'm wiped."

"Never drink and take meds simultaneously," Ken said, winking at her.

"Fine. I want a drink. A stiff one."

"I think I can arrange that." He drove for another five minutes before pulling into a jewelry store's parking lot.

Sam nailed him with a hard look. They'd agreed they'd only get plain gold wedding bands. "What are we doing here?"

"You'll see. Come on." Ken opened his door, and she followed suit. They speed walked into the store.

"Ah, Mr. Zorn, you're here. Let me get it for you," the lady behind the counter said before hurrying to the back of the store.

"The lights make these sparkle," Sam said as she waved at the rings.

Ken made some sort of noise in the back of his throat as he looked at men's watches. The woman came back with a black velvet pad and a small box. "Here we go."

Sam walked over and watched as the woman opened the box, taking out a beautiful firestone opal with two small diamonds on each side. Ken took it from the woman and turned to Sam. "I didn't break my word. I didn't buy this, but I had it reset. This was my mom's engagement ring. I know it's not a big flashy diamond—"

Sam grabbed his face in her hands and kissed his words away. "Thank you. It's beautiful," she said, kissing him again.

When she released him, he slid it on her ring finger. "Can we set a date?" He kissed her again.

"Today?" Sam asked, causing him to laugh.

He shook his head. "Your mother would kill us both."

Sam narrowed her eyes as she looked up at him. "Does it seem like this is more her wedding than ours?"

Ken shook his head. "I love your mom, but I'm not marrying her. If she gets out of hand, I'll talk with her."

Sam rolled her eyes. "She loves you more than me."

"Maybe, but we'll use it as our secret weapon." Ken looked at the woman behind the counter. "Are we square?"

"Absolutely. The receipt is in the bag." She put the ring's case in the bag as well. "Best wishes to both of you."

They darted to the truck, but Sam couldn't help but admire the ring. "This is beautiful."

"I didn't want to say anything until I knew it could be reset." Ken smiled at her. "I do want to set a date. I don't care if you have to take the bar again or a hundred more times. I need you to be my wife."

"I've always wanted a June wedding." Sam chuckled. "I think Mom has the wedding planned. She just needs dates. Kayla said she'd only need a couple of months to rework my mom's dress."

"Pick any day you want. I'll worry about the vacation." Ken smiled at her before pulling out onto the main drag. "It may not be Bali or Fiji, but I have a few dollars put aside."

"Are you sure? We don't need to go anywhere."

"I'm positive. I want you all to myself."

"I think that would be nice." She held up her

hand and admired the changing colors of the white stone. "I couldn't have picked a more perfect ring."

"I couldn't have picked a more perfect woman." Ken reached for her hand and drew it to his lips to kiss it.

The trip back to the hotel was lost to wedding talk. The only thing Ken wanted was the reception at the Bit and Spur's community hall, which was perfect because that was what she wanted, too. Her community had grown since she'd left the troopers. The friendships she'd formed with the women of Hollister was something she'd never had before, well, except for her friend Carol.

Ken opened the door to their hotel room and let her in. She stopped at the doorway. Candles flickered all around the room, and a vase of roses was on a small white-cloth-covered table. The picture was completed with a bucket of champagne, tall, fluted glasses, and a plate of luxurious-looking chocolates.

With all this in her mind, she blurted, "You're not supposed to light candles in a hotel."

Ken laughed and picked up one of the white pillars. He turned it over, and a little bulb and base fell out. "Battery operated."

"This is … why … what … how?" She turned to him.

He shut the door behind them. "Which question do you want me to answer first?" He took off his jacket, and she unzipped hers.

"All of them?"

Taking her jacket, he put it on a chair with his. "This is a celebration of taking the bar. I had all this, minus the flowers, in my truck under the blanket."

"You said that was a cold-weather survival pack."

"Well, it's cold, and we need to survive." He took her by the hand and walked her over to the champagne. "Alex and Kayla swear this is the best chocolate in the world." He lifted the plate, and she took one while he opened the champagne.

She bit into the milk chocolate and groaned as the soft chocolate melted on her tongue immediately. "So good." He handed her a glass of champagne, and she took a sip. "Oh, you have to taste this together." She held the other half of her chocolate for him to take. He lifted it out of her fingers and wound his tongue around them. She shivered. The thrill up her spine was not from the cold.

"Damn," she whispered as she watched him eat the candy.

He took a sip of the champagne, then put down the glass. "I have something else."

"What else could you possibly have?" Ken went into the bathroom and came out sans shirt, boots, and socks. His belt was undone, and the top button of his jeans was open. "Whoa." She gulped another sip of the champagne.

"This." He held up a bottle, and she looked at it. "Warming massage oil." She lifted her eyes to his. "For me?"

"For you. Naked, face down on the bed."

He didn't have to tell her twice. Her clothes went everywhere, and she skittered onto the middle of the bed.

She heard him lose his jeans and took the opportunity to look back at the thick muscles and sexy-as-hell body of the man she loved. His cock was full and heavy. She smiled. It wouldn't be long before the massage became one of her favorite diversions from studying.

She heard the plastic rumble and looked back again to see Ken staring at her as he took the top off the oil. He turned the bottle over …

"Oh, shit!" Sam's legs were covered in oil up

almost to her ass. She squealed and rolled over, jolting the bottle in Ken's hands again, and the oil spilled all over her stomach.

"Get the bedspread off the bed!" Ken said.

Sam jumped up, pulled the bedspread, and then stood on it. She was dripping in oil. She looked down at herself and started laughing. Ken was now standing on the bedspread with a three-quarters-empty bottle of massage oil in his hand. She threw back her head and laughed harder as she closed the space between them. She grabbed him around the waist and slithered her oiled legs and abs against him. "Slippery sex," she murmured.

Ken looked at her and then at the bottle. He turned it upside down and poured it over them before he dropped it on the bedspread. He grabbed her back and tried to control her descent to the floor, but there was so much oil, she slipped out of his grip. She landed on her ass with a resounding thud.

Wide-eyed Sam stared up at him and started laughing again. She lifted her arms and wiggled her fingers. "Come here."

Ken was over her in seconds. They laughed as they fought the slip and slide of the oil and tried to hold onto each other. She rolled onto her stomach, and he covered her. The squelch of the oil between them brought another round of laughter, but that stopped as soon as Ken entered her. She sighed and welcomed him deep inside. He moved a bit to get into a position before he wrapped around her and held her as best as he could. The feel of his lips at the base of her neck and the tender bites he gave to her shoulder sent charges of electricity to her core. She arched as he came forward. The awkward, slippery mess took nothing away from the moment. Ken loved her, and she loved him. The future and plans of weddings, careers, and life were on hold as they made love. When they finished, and Ken slid to one side of her, she turned to him, saying, "I'll never forget this night."

Ken smiled. "Slippery sex?"

"Well, that, and you did all of this for me. You make me feel so special."

"That's because you are. To me, you're everything good and right in the world." He pushed a piece of hair that had escaped her ponytail from her face. "Even when you're covered in oil."

She laughed and lifted her head to look at the bedspread. "We're going to have to pay for this."

Ken smiled and lifted onto his elbow, too.

"That's what credit cards are for, right? Emergencies?"

She nodded. "Absolutely. We should probably wash all this off."

"Shower sex?" Ken's eyebrows lifted comically.

She leaned closer to him. "Mixing oil and water is dangerous, isn't it?"

"Absolutely." He kissed her and lowered her back to the floor. When he pulled away, he said, "We should work some more of this oil off. Safety first."

Sam nodded. "Absolutely. Safety first." She closed her eyes and thanked God for Ken Zorn. He was her peace, her rock, and her world.

EPILOGUE

Barry Marks stood by his pseudo-mom, Corrie Sanchez. She'd loved him like a son, and he loved her, too. Still, he didn't want to be there. The wedding reception was a town event that neither his mother nor Andrew Hollister would let him miss. He swung his gaze over the crowd of people. He hated people. Everyone except Corrie and sometimes Andrew. Speaking of the devil. Andrew Hollister weaved his way through the crowd.

"Corrie, we have a table at the far side. Gen is saving you and Barry a seat."

"Thank you. This is quite a crowd," Corrie noted.

"Alex and Kayla invited the entire county, and I

think everyone showed up," Andrew confirmed. "I want to talk with Barry for a minute. We'll be over soon."

Barry rolled his eyes but smiled at his mom when she looked at him. "I'll be right there," he said. Once Corrie had nodded and made her way through the crush of people, Barry snapped, "We've talked."

Andrew turned on him and was about an inch away from his face when he spoke. "I bailed your ass out of jail and didn't tell her. I'm funding your lawyer. Your anger issues can't be ignored any longer. I will let Corrie know how far down the hole you've fallen if you don't do exactly as I say, and you can go to jail for beating that man half to death."

Barry didn't flinch. He knew he'd fucked up. The rage took over, and when people had pulled him off the guy, he'd thought he'd killed him. He needed help. He needed to do this, but he fucking hated the ax being held over his head. "Right. I understood that the last time we had this conversation."

Andrew held up his hand and lifted a finger. "One, you show up for work Monday morning and bring your kit. You're staying at the bunkhouse.

Two, you will go to appointments with Dr. Wheeler and make each one he schedules. Three, you'll let me, the foreman, or Senior know any time you leave the ranch. All three are non-negotiable."

Barry screwed his jaw together so tightly that his teeth hurt and nodded once. Andrew backed up a step and stared at him. "Your life doesn't have to be spent feeling nothing but hatred and anger."

"Says you," Barry snipped back.

"Says everyone." Andrew threw the response back at him. "This is your one shot, Barry. Your one shot to find a way out of the hell hole your mind is putting you in. Don't throw it away."

Barry didn't respond. Not that Andrew waited around for an answer. He wasn't going to go over to the table right now. He needed a few moments to chew on the fact that Andrew Hollister was a total prick. Barry snorted and shoved his hands into his pockets. That wasn't true. Andrew had answered the phone, and he'd shown up when there was no one left for him to call. Barry watched the line dance happening in front of him. The laughter and smiles were foreign to him. He couldn't remember the last time he'd laughed.

The door behind him opened, and a blast of

cold air entered the dance hall. Barry turned around to glower at the person holding the door open. Instead, he bolted to the door. A woman was leaning against it. Her head was cut, and blood ran down her face. Barry bolted to her, shouting, "We need a doctor!"

The woman slumped as he reached her, and Barry swung her into his arms and turned to the crowd. "We need a fucking doctor, now!" he bellowed, putting an immediate pause to the dancing. A surge of people surrounded him.

"That's Kathy!"

"What happened?"

Barry shook his head. "She opened the door and then passed out."

"God, look at the blood."

"Move, people." Ken Zorn, the sheriff of the county, pushed through the crowd, and a tall blond man followed behind him.

Ken narrowed his eyes at Barry. He knew Barry's history. "Tell me what happened?"

"She opened the door and was bleeding. By the time I got to her, she'd passed out."

"Bring her over here," the doctor said after he lifted her eyelids and felt for a pulse. Barry followed.

"All right, everyone, nothing to see here. Go back to celebrating Kayla and Alex." Ken Zorn held the crowd back.

"She's cold, Doc." Barry could feel the cold radiating off her. "No coat."

"Yeah. Keep a hold of her, Barry." The doctor removed his suit jacket, draped it over Barry's shoulder, and held the other side of the jacket with his free hand, shielding the woman from prying eyes. He moved her dress, and Barry saw a dark red mark across her shoulder and the top of her breast. The doctor looked up and found the sheriff. "Ken, the injuries look like she was in a vehicle accident."

"On it." The man darted out of the dance hall.

Kathy's eyes blinked open, and she stared at Barry.

"Kathy, what happened?" the doctor asked.

The woman didn't move. She simply stared at him. He looked at the doctor and then back at the woman. Barry tried to get through to her and asked, "Kathy, what happened?"

She lifted a hand and touched his cheek. "You didn't do anything wrong. Stop being mad."

Barry's gut clenched. "I'm not mad."

Kathy blinked, and her hand fell away from his

face. She looked over at the doctor. "What happened?"

"That's what we're trying to find out," the doctor said, and he continued to ask questions and look at her injuries. Barry felt the slight figure in his arms start to shiver. He tightened his grip just a bit, trying to keep her warm.

"Barry?"

He blinked and looked over at the doctor. "Yeah?"

"Let's let her sit up now," the doctor repeated himself.

"Oh, sure." He moved her to a chair and carefully placed her on it. The doctor took his coat and put it over Kathy's shoulders.

"Thanks, Barry. I can handle it from here."

Barry nodded and backed away. The woman held out her hand. "Thank you. You're Corrie's son, right?"

"Barry Marks," he replied.

"Barry." She repeated and smiled at him. "Thank you."

He nodded and spun around. The image of that woman's smile stuck in his brain. The only women who smiled at him were the ones who didn't know him. He drew a deep breath and headed to the far corner of the dance hall. He really did not want to be there. Barry stopped and looked back to where the doctor was sitting with Kathy. But ... he was glad he'd been able to help her.

Would you like to read Barry and Kathy's story? Click here!

Did you miss Alex and Kayla's story? Click here!

Join my newsletter here!

ALSO BY KRIS MICHAELS

Kings of the Guardian Series

Jacob: Kings of the Guardian Book 1

Joseph: Kings of the Guardian Book 2

Adam: Kings of the Guardian Book 3

Jason: Kings of the Guardian Book 4

Jared: Kings of the Guardian Book 5

Jasmine: Kings of the Guardian Book 6

Chief: The Kings of Guardian Book 7

Jewell: Kings of the Guardian Book 8

Jade: Kings of the Guardian Book 9

Justin: Kings of the Guardian Book 10

Christmas with the Kings

Drake: Kings of the Guardian Book 11

Dixon: Kings of the Guardian Book 12

Passages: The Kings of Guardian Book 13

Promises: The Kings of Guardian Book 14

The Siege: Book One, The Kings of Guardian Book 15

The Siege: Book Two, The Kings of Guardian Book 16

A Backwater Blessing: A Kings of Guardian Crossover Novella

Montana Guardian: A Kings of Guardian Novella

Guardian Defenders Series

Gabriel

Maliki

John

Jeremiah

Frank

Creed

Sage

Bear

Billy

Guardian Security Shadow World

Anubis (Guardian Shadow World Book 1)

Asp (Guardian Shadow World Book 2)

Lycos (Guardian Shadow World Book 3)

Thanatos (Guardian Shadow World Book 4)

Tempest (Guardian Shadow World Book 5)

Smoke (Guardian Shadow World Book 6)

Reaper (Guardian Shadow World Book 7)

Phoenix (Guardian Shadow World Book 8)

Valkyrie (Guardian Shadow World Book 9)

Flack (Guardian Shadow World Book 10)

Ice (Guardian Shadow World Book 11)

Malice (Guardian Shadow World Book 12)

Harbinger (Guardian Shadow World Book 13)

Hollister (A Guardian Crossover Series)

Andrew (Hollister-Book 1)

Zeke (Hollister-Book 2)

Declan (Hollister- Book 3)

Ken (Hollister - Book 4)

Hope City

Hope City - Brock

HOPE CITY - Brody- Book 3

Hope City - Ryker - Book 5

Hope City - Killian - Book 8

Hope City - Blayze - Book 10

The Long Road Home

Season One:

My Heart's Home

Season Two:

Searching for Home (A Hollister-Guardian Crossover Novel)

Season Three:

A Home for Love (A Hollister Crossover Novel)

STAND-ALONE NOVELS

A Heart's Desire - Stand Alone

Hot SEAL, Single Malt (SEALs in Paradise)

Hot SEAL, Savannah Nights (SEALs in Paradise)

Hot SEAL, Silent Knight (SEALs in Paradise)

Join my newsletter for fun updates and release information!

>>>Kris' Newsletter<<<

ALSO BY KRIS MICHAELS

Kings of the Guardian Series

Jacob: Kings of the Guardian Book 1

Joseph: Kings of the Guardian Book 2

Adam: Kings of the Guardian Book 3

Jason: Kings of the Guardian Book 4

Jared: Kings of the Guardian Book 5

Jasmine: Kings of the Guardian Book 6

Chief: The Kings of Guardian Book 7

Jewell: Kings of the Guardian Book 8

Jade: Kings of the Guardian Book 9

Justin: Kings of the Guardian Book 10

Christmas with the Kings

Drake: Kings of the Guardian Book 11

Dixon: Kings of the Guardian Book 12

Passages: The Kings of Guardian Book 13

Promises: The Kings of Guardian Book 14

The Siege: Book One, The Kings of Guardian Book 15

The Siege: Book Two, The Kings of Guardian Book 16

A Backwater Blessing: A Kings of Guardian Crossover Novella

Montana Guardian: A Kings of Guardian Novella

Guardian Defenders Series

Gabriel

Maliki

John

Jeremiah

Frank

Creed

Sage

Bear

Billy

Guardian Security Shadow World

Anubis (Guardian Shadow World Book 1)

Asp (Guardian Shadow World Book 2)

Lycos (Guardian Shadow World Book 3)

Thanatos (Guardian Shadow World Book 4)

Tempest (Guardian Shadow World Book 5)

Smoke (Guardian Shadow World Book 6)

Reaper (Guardian Shadow World Book 7)

Phoenix (Guardian Shadow World Book 8)

Valkyrie (Guardian Shadow World Book 9)

Flack (Guardian Shadow World Book 10)

Ice (Guardian Shadow World Book 11)

Malice (Guardian Shadow World Book 12)

Harbinger (Guardian Shadow World Book 13)

Hollister (A Guardian Crossover Series)

Andrew (Hollister-Book 1)

Zeke (Hollister-Book 2)

Declan (Hollister- Book 3)

Ken (Hollister - Book 4)

Barry (Hollister - Book 5)

Hope City

Hope City - Brock

HOPE CITY - Brody- Book 3

Hope City - Ryker - Book 5

Hope City - Killian - Book 8

Hope City - Blayze - Book 10

The Long Road Home

Season One:

My Heart's Home

Season Two:

Searching for Home (A Hollister-Guardian Crossover Novel)

Season Three:

A Home for Love (A Hollister Crossover Novel)

STAND-ALONE NOVELS

A Heart's Desire - Stand Alone

Hot SEAL, Single Malt (SEALs in Paradise)

Hot SEAL, Savannah Nights (SEALs in Paradise)

Hot SEAL, Silent Knight (SEALs in Paradise)

Join my newsletter for fun updates and release information!

>>>Kris' Newsletter<<<

ABOUT THE AUTHOR

Wall Street Journal and USA Today Bestselling Author, Kris Michaels is the alter ego of a happily married wife and mother. She writes romance, usually with characters from military and law enforcement backgrounds.

Printed in Great Britain
by Amazon